INDIAN MYTHOLOGY RELOADED

MUCH-LOVED TALES TOLD DIFFERENTLY

DEEPA VAISHNAVI V M

Contents

Samarpane / Dedication *v*

Preface *ix*

Acknowledgements *xi*

Prologue *xv*

1. The Birth 1
2. The Sacrifice 4
3. The Beginning 7
4. The Con 12
5. The Cover 15
6. The Elevation 19
7. The Purge 26
8. The Purification 31
9. The Obeisance 35
10. The Crossing 40
11. The Indicator 45
12. The Wait 49
13. The Games 54
14. The Release 59
15. The Cleansing 63
16. The Shower 68
17. The Lovers 73
18. The Avowal 77
19. The Retrieval 80
20. The Gift 84

Contents

21. The Transgression 88

22. The Satiation 92

23. The Meeting 97

24. The Relief 106

25. The Separation 111

26. The Dispatch 115

27. The Offering 120

The Answers You May Be Seeking 125

Samarpane / Dedication

I present this book at the feet of the divine mother Durga, and to my *ishta devata*, Narasimha. Without their ever-present *krupe* (grace), I could not have written these stories.

•

This book is dedicated to my parents, Smt. Usha Madhuranathan and Shri. V V Madhuranathan, and to my brothers Shri. Ravi Kiran and Chi. Praveen. It is no exaggeration when I say, I am what I am today because of them.

•

I also dedicate this book to the countless nameless writers, and the many well-known authors of the various works of Indian mythology, through the ages. It is from their works that I draw inspiration.

***

करमण्येवाधिकारस्तेमाफलेषुकदाचन।
माकरमफलहेतुर्भूर्मातेसंगोऽस्त्वकरमणि॥

- *Bhagawad Gita*, Chapter 4, Verse 37.

ꢁ

In the first week of May 1989, when I was about to appear for the second round of the NTSE Examination, my father recited this shloka to me and said, 'Do your best and leave the rest to God.' His words have remained with me to this day.

Preface

Ten years ago, on 10 May 2012, something compelled me to write a short poem, titled 'Deliverance', and I shared it with my friends on Facebook. An ode to my beloved god Narasimha, it did not name any character. However, if one knew the story of Prahalada, they were sure to understand what was being described.

That evening, my cousin Divya called me and over a long conversation, encouraged me to write more and publish more often. Unknown to her, she was amplifying my mother's stated desire. I'm sure there was some divine intervention as well! Thus began my journey of retelling some well-known and much-loved tales from the epics *Ramayana and Mahabharata*, and the *Puranas*.

I grew up listening to these stories – initially, when my paati (grandmother) or Amma narrated them, and later, reading them –thanks to the countless Amar Chitra Katha books that I devoured regularly. That Amma used to arrange dolls during the Sharan Navaratri each year based on themes and stories from our Puranas was an added advantage, as it helped me visualise these stories from a three dimensional perspective.

A story would suddenly pop into my mind, and I would type it out. The first person I would read it to was Amma. The next thing I would do was share it with my friends on social media. Soon it became a puzzle for readers to solve - who is the narrator, what is the story, who are the other characters. As guesses – many valid, others wild –

populated the comments section, I had several enjoyable interactions with friends and acquaintances.

This book is but an attempt to share with readers some of the 50-odd stories I've written so far. This book is also to commemorate my parents wedding anniversary which is on 3rd June.

I hope you enjoy reading these stories as much as I enjoyed penning them.

Acknowledgements

It is due to the help, support, and contribution of some very special people that this book is being published. I am deeply grateful to each of them.

First and foremost, my mother, guide and god, Smt. Usha Madhuranathan, who was the first one to read the story every time I wrote a new one. It is in her memory that I am publishing this book.

My *chithi* (auntie / maasi), Smt. Pushpa Raghuram, who, over these past few years, constantly reminded me that my stories were awaiting publication, and who, along with Shri. M G Raghuram, stood by me like a rock during the most difficult period of my life.

My cousin, nay sister, Divya Raghuram, who has been my critic, friend, confidant, and more all these years.

Shruti Vidyasagar, another cousin who is also a very dear sister, a friend and the go-to person for so many things. Shri. T R Vidyasagar, who has been a wonderful source of support on various matters for years now. And the dear ones, Nidhi and Nilufer, who have honoured me with the title 'Doddamma'.

Meera K, a friend, mentor, and boss – a person I look up to – who has also given me many opportunities to write professionally for over a decade now.

Dr. Kalyanasundaram Seshadri and Dr. Priya Kayastha who have been guiding and encouraging me these past few years, and helping me grow as a person.

Girish Shenoy, who is not just my rakhi brother but also someone who has been an amazing support to Amma and I over the years.

Raksha Sriram, Smt. Jyothi Mohan and Shri. Mohan Prabandam, Prithvi Bhaktapriya, Nandita Ashok, Anasuya Rao, Arathi P Balaji, Harish N, Smt. E V Lakshmi, and Shri. E K Chari, and Vani Deshikachar – people who have been there for me consistently, caring for me, rooting for me.

Shri. Eswar Sarma and Shri. MVRK Sastry – my English teachers from KVVSP, and Ma'am John (from NMKRV), who inspired in me the love of English as a language.

Members of my Tirumalai and Vankipuram families, who love(d) writing and reading, especially my maternal aunt, Miss Sampath (Smt. T S Rukmayi) and my paternal grandfather, Shri. V S Venkatakrishnaswami. As also my auntie, Smt. Suma Seshadri aka Krishna.

Mrudula Ravi Kiran, who diligently helped me with the publishing process and other related activities.

My friend Aparna Rajagopalan, who agreed to help me illustrate this book, and my dear childhood friend and confidant Jaya (Roy) Parbat, who has also contributed to the illustrations. Both did so at very short notice.

Hemanth N of Canvasay, for the book cover and a couple of illustrations – we literally worked on this till the last minute.

Vinay Nagaraju, Jayashree P K, Venkataprasad B, and the many friends I have made over the years at Landmark, for their valuable friendship.

All my Facebook 'friends' who read my stories there and encouraged me to write more. These include family members, and online friends, many of whom I am yet to meet.

Smt. Meenali Joshi of GFWMJ, my wellness coach, who gently coached me into working on this book, especially when I was doubtful about completing it within the deadline I had set for myself.

Smt. Jayamma and Smt. Yashoda, the two wonderful ladies who helped Amma, and are now helping me, with the household chores for over a decade now. As also Shri Thippeswamy, Smt. Jayalakshmi and Smt. Saraswati at my aunt's place.

A heartfelt 'thank you' to each of the above. And to anyone else I may have unwittingly missed.

And to you, the reader of this book.

Deepa Vaishnavi V M
Bengaluru, India
25 May 2022

Prologue

'Another book on Indian Mythology? How is it any different from the others?'

I will not be surprised if that was your first thought when you came upon this book. For indeed, there are so many books on this topic right now. From children's books to those more suitable for adults.

This book is somewhere in the middle. To begin with, one needs to know some of the main stories from our epics to be able to appreciate this one. Next, since no story has been 'directly' narrated, it would be more suitable for young adults and others from the point of view of comprehension and content. Further, this book is not suitable for children, especially those who are yet to be introduced to stories from the puranas and the epics.

Back to the basics first. Epics such as the Ramayana and Mahabharata consist of many stories and sub-plots. The various antics of Krishna, be it overpowering the snake Kaali or lifting the Govardhana mountain, the valour of Rama, or the penance of Shiva, are all familiar stories that have been narrated to children by their elders through generations. And these stories have usually been told in the third person, and with names of the characters and the locations clearly specified.

I wanted to rewrite these tales from a different perspective. In most of these stories, the protagonist is not a living being. In fact, the protagonist or narrator could be something (or someone) mentioned merely in passing in the traditional telling of the stories. So, my narrator could be an axe, a garland of flowers, the threshold, or any other thing that witnessed the actions featuring characters such as Rama, Krishna, Draupadi, and Karna.

What's also different is that names of characters and locations are alluded to, and not stated explicitly. Also, the identity of the narrator is not revealed till almost the end of the story, adding an element of surprise.

As I wrote these stories, I saw that there were so many nuances to black and white, right and wrong, good and bad. I understood that various interpretations are possible of the tales we grew up with, whose meanings and conclusions we took for granted. I have since started looking for different angles to narrate a familiar story.

Although the stories in this book are short, I recommend you don't hurry through them. Experience the emotions, visualise its characters, think of a familiar tale that could be related, recollect the incident associated with the tale you know, identify the narrator – if you can! – and then proceed to the next story.

Deepa Vaishnavi V M
Bengaluru, India
25 May 2022

I

The Birth

The battle was fierce.

Each side was as powerful as the other.

Neither was willing to step back or cede. Neither was willing to listen to counsel. There was too much at stake.

Onlookers shivered in fear while also staring in awe, albeit from a safe distance.

This was a battle like no other. One without precedent. One that would never be fought again. In fact, no one had imagined that such a battle would ever take place.

A mere '**No**' had been the first weapon in this epic battle which was between... obedience and ego, determination and stubbornness, creative power and destructive ability. ignorance and arrogance, fearlessness and power, commitment and anger... A young one and the ageless.

The sheer intensity of the battle sent shivers down the spine of the bravest of brave. So petrified was each onlooker that no one dared step in to attempt a ceasefire.

.

A glint of metal. A powerful whizzing sound. A defiant target.

And then...

Total silence!

.

Not a thing or person moved. It was as if time had stood still.

As the insolent victor watched, out walked the person who had unwittingly caused this battle, and who was unaware of it all till now.

One glance was all it took for that person to grasp what had occurred.

And anger found a new expression...

Silence had never been so deafening! Or so frightful.

.

With dread writ large on their faces, the onlookers waited for the inevitable explosion.

The Earth shivered in agony. Water gushed out and flowed everywhere. Fires soared heavenward as if fuelled by grief. Winds bellowed in pain. Space trembled...

Nature had revolted against the killing of an innocent one, and it was not going to be easy to calm her down.

.

The onlookers scattered like dust. No one wanted to be in the line of fire of a battle that was certain to commence any moment now. A battle that would be many times more dreadful than the one they had just witnessed, for it would be between two parallel powers.

.

Yet...

Redemption was possible only if the dead was brought back to life.

And so it happened...

The head of a pachyderm, and the title "Leader of the Multitude" were affixed.

And thus came to life...

The steadfast faith in countless hearts that, when there is an obstacle, there will be a force beyond comprehension to help them vanquish it.

Vighnaharata Shri Ganesha!

II

The Sacrifice

The flames engulf him.

And his thoughts race back in time. To where it all started...

'Love' is his middle name. He is, after all, *the* expert. Carefree and frivolous, he is loved by all. He has just shared an extremely satisfactory kiss with his beautiful consort when the summons arrive.

Everyone knows he is lethal and always effective. He has not yet missed a single target. Working alone most of the time, and with seemingly harmless weapons, he has overpowered each and everyone assigned to him. A very discreet operator, his presence is hardly, if at all ever, felt.

Stealth is his modus operandi.

There is a hitch though. He has not yet tested his might against the one who lives, by choice, like an ascetic, and whom no one has ever been able to reach. At least, not for a very long time now.

And today, the time has come.

The Council of Elders has decided that he should go. Seek out the lone one and do his job. The consensus is that no one else could be as effective as he.

His own father has approved this particular assignment. The most risk-filled one ever.

If he succeeds, he will be remembered forever as the one who achieved the impossible. If he fails...the consequences are too grave to even think about, the least of them being his total annihilation.

He *has* to succeed. There is too much at stake.

He does not believe in premonitions. Yet...

He embraces his wife and bids her goodbye – he has never done that before, say 'Goodbye', that is.

Worry and pride fight for a place in her eyes. He walks away without waiting to see which wins. Nothing that would weaken his resolve must be encouraged.

He sets out.

It is spring, the season that brings him great joy. His work is always easier when Spring is around. Today, the flowers are doubly fragrant, as if in anticipation of something momentous. And the bees...they are raring to go, their hum music to his ears.

His chosen mode of transport takes flight. And very soon, they have left behind all habitation.

As he nears the mountains where the ascetic is believed to live, he experiences a hitherto unknown feeling – as if the cold hand of death is gleefully caressing his backbone. He shivers in dread but resolutely ploughs on.

The mountain mists, which till then were playing hide and seek with him, vanish all of a sudden.

The target is in sight. Seated on a rock – eyes closed – as if deep in thought.

As he draws closer, his hands go numb. He is assailed by fear. He trembles and almost turns back. Almost...

Gathering courage, he sneaks up to his target. Honour forbids him from attacking from behind.

Invoking the gods, a first for him, he raises his bow. Taking careful aim, he releases the arrow. The very next instant, it finds its target.

What was intended by the Council has been achieved.

The ascetic's penance is broken. For ever. He is finally roused from a grief-induced state of detachment – he now has nothing to hold on to. Not even his grief...

Enraged at this loss, the ascetic opens an eye – a single eye – the eye that holds in it the power to destroy.

From his third eye emerges the energy that had been building up inside him all this while, ever since he started his horrendous penance. Manifesting as a beam of intense red flame, it shoots towards the culprit – the one who released the arrow – the one who is synonymous with desire.

The flames engulf this epitome of love and he turns to ash.

And a whole new chapter commences...

III

The Beginning

I am the choosen one!

She will be here anytime now. And we shall become one.

We have been dancing the dance of love for days now – playing the ritualistic mating game – furtive glances, accidental touches, and coy smiles.

And today...today, we shall be taking it to its most beautiful and inevitable conclusion.

The spot I have chosen for our coming together could not be more beautiful or serene. Surrounded by towering trees, the leaves forming a natural curtain, the countless beautiful and fragrant flowers...it is indeed paradise. What more could one ask for?

My heart is galloping in excitement. I can barely wait.

.

My dear. Where are you?

.

Is the spot I have chosen too far away? Here, in this forest, we would be safe and away from curious eyes. Or so I thought. Am I mistaken? Is it fear of discovery that is keeping you away?

.

Oh! Why are you doing this to me? Why are you not here yet?

Has something held you back?

Have you changed your mind?

.

Have you found someone more suitable? But that cannot be possible – I am the best! And you know it!

.

I am no scholar – I cannot spout poetry at will. You know that I am a child of the wild, and that my love is as real and passionate.

Yet...

.

Am I not good enough for you?

Handsome or strong enough?

.

Was it all only a game for you?

Have you been blind to my love?

.

Oh! You are so cruel.

You seem to find great pleasure in taunting me thus. Not coming at the appointed time!

.

Squirrel – do not mock me by scampering around thus, imitating my actions.

Gentle deer – your eyes accuse me of being too passionate. Being in love too much.

Oh beautiful butterflies – don't fly away from me like that – as if I were a lion letting out a roar. It is disappointment that is making me cry out.

.

Wait a minute!

There are so many dangerous beasts and men around – wild animals, dacoits, hunters, elephants...

My heart. My beloved! Have you fallen prey to one of them? I hope not.

Oh my LORD! I beseech you. Let that not be. Please protect my beloved. Please. PLEASE! She is too valuable to me – I cannot live a second without her. Not anymore. I love her too much...

The silence mocks me.

The stillness scares me.

The breeze brings me your scent!...

Ah! There you are, my love.

More beautiful and graceful than ever. Pure as white with just the merest hint of black lining your eyes. The love in them, encompassing me. Overpowering me. Drowning me.

I can see your heart beat. Feel your breath.

Don't stop there. Come closer. Closer. Even more. Closer. Close...

You are a tease!

Just when I thought I had you in my embrace, you slip away.

Wait my dear. I am coming right after you.

We love birds will soar in the skies – free and unfettered. Something beautiful and magnificent will be born as a result of our pure love.

AHHHHHHHHHHH.................................

The pain! It is intolerable!

Where did that arrow come from? It has pierced right through me! There is blood everywhere. My breath is failing me.

My dear. Don't cry. Oh, please don't cry.

Hurry! Go away before you too are shot. Someone is coming this way. Go away. Go...

What is it that I hear? Who is that speaking? Is that the human who gets his name from an anthill?

What is he saying to that heartless hunter who shot me on the sly?

मा नषिाद प्रतष्ठिां त्वमगमश्शाश्वतीस्समा: ।
यत्क्रौञ्चमथिुनादेकमवधी: काममोहतिम् ।।

"Ma nishad pratishtha tvamgamah shashvati samaha
Yatkraunch mithunadekhamvadhi kammohitam"

"O Hunter! Denounced throughout the world shall you be forever.

For, you have separated two lovelorn birds forever!"

The Gods be praised. That is a couplet he has voiced in his grief - in my grief - in our grief, my beloved.

.

The world will be blessed now. With a tale that will be written and narrated for ever and ever.

.

Indeed, I am the chosen one...

.

.

.

IV

The Con

"So be it."

Simple words uttered by someone so powerful that destiny was rewritten in an instant.

I cannot help but marvel at how one ordinary person could make the setting sun rise - retrace its path...metaphorically speaking, that is.

A once-in-a-lifetime event – our lifetime, at least, as I have not seen anything like this happen ever since...

I am synonymous with the master I serve.

Together, we perform a critical task that no one else likes doing. The irony is that everyone dislikes us because of that.

It does not matter to us though. We have long gotten used to all the negativity that is invariably directed towards us. There are a few here and there, and every now and then, who appreciate what we do, but they do so only because it serves some vested interest of theirs. We do not care for them either.

It is not that our work is without perks. We travel a lot, and have enjoyed visiting some of the most beautiful places that exist. Be it a snow-clad mountain or the seashore, the valley of flowers or a river's basin, a beautiful city or the peaceful forest – we have been there all.

It was during one such jaunt that we met our match. To say that we were very cleverly outwitted would be an understatement.

We had completed our business for the day and were on our way back home. Given the beauty and serenity of the place, we had taken the longer route.

We usually travel alone. But on that day, we had company, a beautiful lady.

So bewitching was she, that, she could have easily put to shame some of the most beautiful women of the world. Complementing her beauty was the depth of knowledge she possessed, and her ability to converse.

So intelligent was she that we often found it difficult to keep up with her in the conversation between her and our master which was, by the way, both entertaining and challenging.

The conversation soon took the form of a competition. The loser of each round had to give the victor something that the latter wished for.

We knew what she wanted, and we were very clear that our master would not give it to her.

The only way he could justly deny her was by winning the competition while also setting the condition that she will not ask for the one thing that he was not going to give.

She readily agreed to the condition.

Our master should have actually been on his guard then and there. But alas... To this day I wonder why he never saw the trap he was slowly walking into...

The conversation continued.

Each argument of hers was so convincing that my master, who is considered one of the most knowledgeable ones ever, could not help but cede each round to her.

In return, she asked that her father-in-law's eyesight, and kingdom be restored.

"So be it," said my master.

Next, she asked for sons for her father.

"So be it," said my master.

She then asked for sons for herself so that the lineage of the family she had married into could continue.

"So be it," said my master.

Only as the final boon left his lips did he realize that, for her to have sons, her husband had to be with her. And we were taking away her husband...

I had, just before the lady began walking with us, pulled his soul out from his body. That had been our business for the day.

And so it came to pass, the steadfast commitment of one person made the setting sun rise... and return life to a soulless body. She would thereafter be revered as one of the most devoted wives who ever lived - the one who dared to follow Death and bring her dead husband back to life.

ꕥ

V

The Cover

My job is to protect.

Without me or my ilk, many would not be able to survive in this harsh world – well, at least not during their initial days.

We have been created with the specific purpose of protecting those entrusted in our care. And that is our one and only duty.

We are fragile, yet strong. We possess within us great potential - for life, for strength, and for all things big and small. From the moment we are created, each of us is assigned one specific being, and our responsibility towards them is immense and lifelong - well, at least as long as we live.

Not for a moment can we allow our loyalties to shift – not even for a split second. The truth is, from the time we are created, we become attached to the one assigned to us. It is our bounden duty to take care of them till they are ready to face the world. The duration of our care varies though – a few days, a few months, a few years, or, very rarely, a few decades.

We live and die for the ones we safeguard. It may interest you to know that the second the duration of our care ends, we die.

.

I have been on duty for a thousand years now. And during this period, I have witnessed many important events taking place, many of them not pleasant.

I have seen the relationship between two sisters deteriorate beyond mere sibling rivalry.

I have heard stories of the great churning. And of the poison the three-eyed one holds in his throat. I have also heard about the divine coming together of the one who rests on a serpent bed, and his beautiful consort who is the daughter of the ocean.

I have also been a mute witness to the destruction of my brother. I have watched helplessly and yet thankfully, as the person who destroyed my brother was cursed. I say thankfully for the sole reason that, as a result of that curse, I have been spared from a similar premature end.

.

The world is a very strange place. And relationships stranger still.

I have been witness to a mother being cursed by a son. I have also heard whispers of how another mother cursed her many strong and powerful children to a painful death. In fact, it has also been rumoured that she used them to trick her own sister into losing a bet. No one speaks about it though for fear of being silenced permanently - through a snake bite.

.

While I have seen negative aspects in relationships, I have seen various beautiful moments too.

Truth be told, I am very grateful to the love and devotion with which I have been taken care of by the lady to whom I was gifted all those years ago. Despite her current lack of freedom, she has ensured that I stay protected from any harm. I am happy in the knowledge that, while I cannot help her personally, the one I am currently protecting will be the one who will relieve her from her state of servitude to one younger than her.

I have felt her pain and her hope, every time she has caressed me with love. Her tears have often silently bathed me, while her barely expressed words have vibrated through my entire being. Her heartfelt prayers have strengthened my core by the minute.

.

Let us not forget the one I have been assigned to shield. He has been growing in strength each day. Any day now, he will break out of his shell and redeem his mother from the clutches of her manipulative sibling.

I can hear the hissing nearby – something I have grown used to for a long time now.

.

Wait a moment...

.

What is this?

I am suddenly feeling warm from within. It is as if a fire has been lit inside me. I am starting to glow.

It is as if something powerful in unfurling within me.

.

"Argh!!!"

.

The pain is unbearable. I can take it no more. I feel as if my insides are being clawed at. Pecked.

Unable to resist the force within me any longer, I break open.

And out comes the most spectacular bird ever. The one who will be soon declared as the king of birds.

The one who will take his mother's name and will be known as the son who freed his mother from servitude. The one who will have many names but will serve only one master.

Even as I shatter into countless pieces, I see him rise from my fold. He glows like fire and has the power to vanquish almost anyone and everyone. His mere presence sends shivers down the spines of his many spineless reptilian step-brothers.

As I start to breathe my last, a flash of insight tells me that he will be so powerful that, an entire clan will forever live in fear. He will be the only one to have the distinction of not only being the mount of the lord, but also of flying above him, albeit as his flag. He will forever be the one to whom people will bow first before seeking his lord's grace.

As for me, I am blessed to have borne, within me, this amazing being. Through him, I have attained salvation.

VI
The Elevation

I am of no consequence.

I am but a lowly part of a larger whole. A branch in a tree. A piece of wood in a frame. A building in a city...

On my own, my existence is of little value. On the other hand, along with others, and on the whole, I can be formidable - even hold an enemy at bay, if need be.

Well, that is what I believe. The others with me do not seem to care much though, either about my existence, or the lack of it should that happen. Why? Because, unlike them, I hardly shoulder any responsibility. In fact, they think the burden we all carry together rests totally with them and therefore have no time for a mere cog in the wheel that I am.

Enough about my feeling of inferiority. Let me tell you a little about what has been happening for a while now. Mind you, I have not always been a witness to the various events that have unfolded these past few years. I have however heard a lot of stories that have been doing the rounds.

The first incident that was literally earth shaking was that a beloved brother was chased and gored to death. His siblings thirst for revenge to this day.

Subsequently, a lady was attacked by a sly being while her husband was away. Providence ensured that she was rescued before she lost her life. Her child was however affected – afflicted, some may say.

Improbable boons were sought and granted. The balance of power tilted towards the side of evil.

Arrogance ruled.

Fear had been set loose, and it gleefully feasted on the hearts of all. Soon, anger became the right of one person alone, and he used it at will, and against anyone he disliked. People were petrified of him and his cohorts. There was nowhere to hide, and no one to protect them.

Despotism had found a new kingdom – the entire world.

The reign of terror appeared to have no end. No one could escape from its vicious clutches. Not even the little ones. Not even the one I love...

My acquaintance with the little one began when he was first brought home.

His innocence appealed to me. He would often come to me and play by my side. I would watch over him, and soon, without realizing it, began caring for him.

A self-willed child, loved though he was by his parents, he was not disposed to follow their instructions most times.

A forthright child, he would say what was on his mind, and do what he liked. As a consequence, he has had his share of adventures too! Poisoned food, venomous snakes, tremendous heights, raging fires, dangerous weapons, elephants in musth... he has lived through them all.

I have not been a witness to most (mis)adventures, but have heard enough aghast whispers to know that the child has survived all this, and more. What is interesting though is that, no matter what happens, that enchanting smile of his has never parted company with him. Ever. Nor has his steadfast conviction.

In a battle of wills, he has been winning– each time.

.

Today has dawned no different from yesterday. Conversations I have heard so far are similar to the ones I have been listening to for some time now.

Nothing has changed. Nothing reduced. Be it the anger or the fear. The aggression or the agitation. The stubbornness or the hatred. The thirst for vengeance or the deep-seated desire to dominate. The frustration or the desperation.

The love or the devotion...

They have all, on the contrary, increased and continue to grow by leaps and bounds.

All the aforementioned negativity is bouncing off the walls with a vehemence that is shaking us to the core. All of us are trembling wondering what is going to happen next.

.

And all of a sudden...

I feel a strange vibration run through me! It is as if something very powerful has me in its grip...some strange sensation fills me, making me feel light and bright. Some strange power zips from one side to another, causing each atom and molecule within me to hum.

The vibrations increase by the second. It is as if this strange and surprisingly angry power has now taken me over completely, and is waiting to burst out. I look around and see a strange glow everywhere even though it is dusk, and the sun has just set.

I spot the owner of the abode of which I am a part saying something to the little one, bellowing at him in rage, his eyes blood-shot, and his grip on his weapon, deathlike. Such is the anger a father is displaying towards his own son!

The vibrations gather speed.

.

"WHERE is your saviour? **IN THIS PILLAR???**"

.

A mace hits a pillar near me, and in the blink of an eye, the strange power possessing me lets go. And before I can even begin to comprehend the loss, the pillar shatters into pieces. And out comes...

.

The most unnerving and magnificent being one has ever seen ...

.

Neither man nor animal. Neither born nor created. Neither a known god nor a demon. Nary a weapon but for the razor-sharp claws! The roar that issues forth from this bewildering and horrific manifestation is blood-curdling! The rage, palpable.

.

The tyrannical father is stupefied into inaction. And before he can recover his senses, with another spine-chilling roar, this lion-headed being picks him up and...starts walking towards me!

.

He sits on me and places the dazed father on his lap. The latter is now neither on the ground nor in the air. And because of my location, he is neither within the abode nor without...

And as the son looks on, his lord proceeds to disembowel the father with those claws. Setting him free for the first time in the process.

And then, the lord turns and looks at his ardent devotee – the little one. And smiles! The love overflowing from the lord's eyes can only be experienced – not described.

.

The entire world rejoices at the death of the oppressor.

.

As for me, I am in a state of bliss.

The omnipresent had made me his abode for a short while. He thereafter elevated me to a position of worship by making me his seat.

I and my ilk will forever be worshiped by believers henceforth.

ꕥ

.
.
.
.
.
.

ꕥ

Deliverence
(the poem that started it all)

.

The silence
The placidity
The vibrancy
The dichotomy
The waiting...

The boy and the man
The son and the king
The believer and the atheist
The unshakable faith and the unbridled anger

Evening sliding into dusk
Anger exploding into rage
Faith turning into certainty

The all pervasive
The one with unlimited power

waits...

A striking blow to a pillar
And a maniac invites his end

An explosion of light
Silence shattered by a reverberating roar
As the sun slips into the loving folds of the horizon

Neither day nor night
Neither man nor animal
Neither within nor without
Neither weapons nor hand

An abdomen torn open
And entrails become a garland
A cursed soul attains liberation
The universe rejoices at its deliverance
And the lion god... smiles.

ꕥ

ꕥ

VII

The Purge

The gurgling river. The melodious nightingale. The gentle deer... The woods are so peaceful today.

.

I lie on the rocks basking in the sun while my friend enjoys his swim in the river.

It is like almost any other day in this part of the forest where, every morning, we collect firewood and fruits for the day. That has been our routine for days. Weeks. Years. In fact, from the time we became friends.

.

No songs will ever be composed about our friendship. But then, who needs them? We have been creating our own music for a long time now. I provide the rhythm to his songs.

The trees in the woods are silent witnesses to our friendship. People talk about the two of us with reverence, and just a little bit of fear.

.

It was his fervent desire to be a warrior par excellence that brought me into his life.

We were introduced to each other by the Master from whom he had sought the knowledge of warfare. Instantaneously, we formed a bond of friendship that has since strengthened day after day. And it is this bond that is seeing us through these troubled times.

.

For, unfortunately, there is anarchy, debauchery and terror all around.

Lands are being ravaged and innocent people are being tortured in ways so savage that even thinking about what the hapless populace is enduring makes one shiver in fear, and pray that they will not be targeted next.

Fear and prayer have become the way of life for the common man. As also a fatalistic acceptance of atrocities being committed, and loss of life and limb.

Most probably, since we have been living near the woods, we have been spared all this. Well, at least till very recently.

.

I shall never forget that day...

.

Blood. Warm and red. Gushing out from the neck of a noble lady – my friend's mother. Her lifeless body lying at my friend's feet.

Woe be on me – for I was the one instrumental in her beheading!

I have always been the unrelenting one – harsh and unyielding – while he has been the one with heart. Yet, that day, for a while, it appeared as if we had interchanged qualities.

I did not know how to deal with my guilt. What was worse was not knowing how to reduce my friend's grief. But not once did he blame me. With a stoicism of which I had been unaware, he went about doing what had to be done.

And things seemed to settle down...

.

But that is not when the trouble started. The trouble started today when, in return for our heartfelt and generous hospitality, the man who was supposed to take care of his citizens, instead stole from us our very precious and revered family member.

How could we tolerate this gross violation of our family? So off we went, my friend and I, and engaged the kidnapper in a battle. We finally chopped off the head of this unrelenting and egoistic ruler – he with the strength of a thousand arms – and brought back our loved one.

And right now, we are at the river, having just cleansed ourselves of the vile blood of the selfish and inconsiderate monarch of the land, and attempting to enjoy the peace and calm that seems to have settled all around...

.

What is this heart-wrenching plaintive cry that we hear?

My friend's name!

Being called by someone in severe pain.

.

The silence and peace are shattered! And I get the feeling that it will be a very long time before we acquaint ourselves with peace again.

.

Reaching out, my friend pulls me up, and we rush towards our dwelling place.

.

And what do we find?

.

A holy space, which till then housed the sacred fire, is now strewn with decapitated bodies! Of my friend's father and brothers.

A place which used to have the fragrance of flowers, camphor and sandal wafting through the air, now reeks of blood.

A hermitage, which would reverberate with holy chants, is now eerily silent except for the intermittent sobbing of the lady whose husband and sons have been brutally massacred.

This brave lady, with her husband's head on her lap, looks up at my friend, and says, "Go my dear child. And avenge the deaths. Not of your father and brothers. But of righteousness, peace and justice. Evil and the vices have reared their ugly heads long enough – they need to be destroyed before people stop believing in all things good."

•

A noble lady indeed. For she is the same one who was beheaded a few days ago upon instructions from her husband, and subsequently brought back to life because of my friend's absolute obedience to his father.

•

I look at my friend. His eyes are bloodshot and brimming with tears of rage. Finding his loved ones killed as a senseless act of revenge for the just death of a tyrannical ruler makes his blood boil.

The frustration and anger that had been lying dormant all these days spill out. He rises to his feet like a wounded snake getting ready to strike. He fumes like a volcano that is about to erupt.

•

As we set off to seek those who caused this carnage, I can feel the thirst for revenge and blood vibrate from my friend's hand.

I alone will ever know the force and angst with which my friend gripped me when he first came face to face with the assassins – the sons of the dead ruler. And then, as one, we set about systematically annihilating each of them.

As a petrified observer would later recall, "*He was like a one-man army. He and his axe. Together, and in the blink of an eye, they laid waste an entire clan.*"

.

The purpose of our existence is starting to unfold. With each person being felled, I rejoice. Our life would be, for a long time to come, dedicated to eliminating evil from this wonderful earth.

And from this moment onward, my friend will forever have my name prefixed to his.

.

The odyssey of cleansing has just commenced. Much 'royal' blood will flow before our purpose is served.

My friend and I will continue to bathe in blood for a long time before we part.

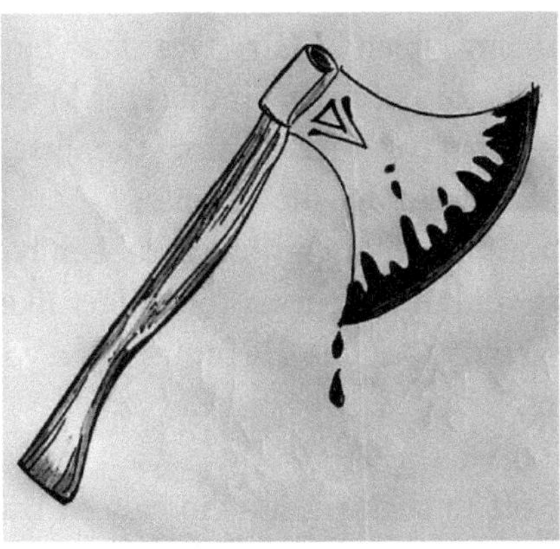

VIII

The Purification

We are waiting.
She is waiting.
He cannot wait any longer.

Despair, patience and penitence have been our companions.
For a long time now.
Patience is not a virtue she has.
Yet, she has had to wait. For ages.
He does not have time to be patient.
Not even a moment.

We have led a glorious life.
She has had a glorious birth.
He is yet to achieve his glory.

Our arrogance has caused us and our loved ones great anguish.
Her arrogance is yet to be moulded into humility.
He cannot afford arrogance.

One mistake, and we have been reduced to a state of total dependence on someone else.

One slip-up and she could be bound or imprisoned.

One blunder and everything he has worked for all these days could turn to dust.

We have nowhere to go, nothing to prove.
She has an important journey to undertake.
He has to guide her to her destination.

Repentance.
Readiness.
Responsibility.

Our predicament.
Her promise.
His penance.

And finally, the boon.

Our wait is about to end.
Her journey begins.
His odyssey continues.

In excitement and joy, she commences her travel. Rushing alongside him.

White and glorious, she is beauty and power personified. Finally free to express herself, she moves like a child rushing out to discover hitherto unexplored territories. Like the hatchling that has just discovered that it can soar in the skies.

She is the glowing ember that has burst into flames.

She is the bubbling lava that has burst through the hitherto dormant volcano.

She is the fearful gale that has torn away everything in its path.

.

The thundering noise.
The force of the fall.
The deluge.

.

All fail to evoke fear in his heart.

.

Exuberant, and arrogant, she rushes to overpower the one who is an embodiment of power and destruction. A very foolish move for she is, very easily and magnificently, controlled, restricted, subdued.

.

And we wait. In anticipation.

.

A little wiser, she sets off again. This time, he has to race ahead of her in order to ensure that she does not go astray. Playfully, she meanders here and there. Dancing to her own tune. Still slightly over-confident.

.

Another encounter.
Another subjugation.
Another release.

.

And we wait. Praying like we never have before.

.

He leads her. To us.

.

And finally, we are immersed ... in joy, in gratitude, in love. And, released from the curse.

He attains fame for posterity.

While she flows on...cleansing the sins of the countless.

.
.
.

Ganga cleansing the ashes of Bhagiratha's ancestors

IX

The Obeisance

I am formidable.

Handsome, tall and sturdy as a tree, and slim like a serpent, my mere presence has sent darts of fear through the hearts of many brave hearts.

One of an extremely elite group, I have served only one master till date. At some point of time, he asked a king to take care of me, and I have been with the latter's family for generations now.

I am currently housed in the luxurious abode of a noble soul. All my needs are being taken care of very well, and with total devotion. And with just a tinge of trepidation, if I may add.

I await instructions on what I am to do next.

Over the years, while those who serve me – brave warriors and the cleaning staff included – are still in awe of me, I have been won over by the innocence and charm of the daughter of the house.

While others would stay away from me whenever possible, this little one would come over and include me in many of her childish games. As she blossomed into youth,

I gradually became a friend to her – one she could hide behind during a hide and seek game, confide in whenever she felt the need, or just sit with when she needed some silent contemplation time.

.

I do not know exactly when I started feeling as protective of her as her father. Along with the paternal feelings of care and concern grew in me the wish that she find a life partner who was worthy of her.

My joy knew no bounds when, one fine day, her father announced that those aspiring to seek her hand in marriage would have to wrestle with me first.

An auspicious day for the contest was identified, and my wait commenced. I wanted only the best of the best for my little girl.

.

The designated day finally dawned. And it was a beautiful one. The flowers were in full bloom and the sun was shining gently down on the earth, as if blessing one and all. The entire city was decorated like a bride. People had thrown open their houses and hearts to the visitors. For, after all, today was the day when the beloved daughter of their land would choose her partner.

I was ready and looking forward to the day's proceedings, till...

.

As had been her daily practice for years, my princess came to meet me. She bowed down to me in reverence and started speaking. As usual. What was different though was that, for the first time today, with a slight shiver in her subdued voice, she whispered to me her heart's desire. Something that disturbed me...

My little one had grown up all of a sudden. She had chosen a partner for herself. And she had just told me who he was.

What worried me was that, from her description of him, I was certain the lad would not be able to overpower me. I was not even sure if he would be allowed to compete.

But, alas! There was not a thing I could do about it. Not a thing!

On one hand, I was bound by my host's condition – I could not go against it. On the other, I could not do anything that would compromise my integrity. If I did, I would be destroying the credibility of my entire clan. No one would ever trust any of us again, ever!

It was thus with a very heavy heart I allowed myself to be led out a while later.

•

Needless to say, I was given a position of prime importance. Visible to everyone, in all my glory.

Aspirants from far and near had gathered at the designated place much before the appointed time. Each eager to win over the hand of the beautiful maiden. And each eager to show off to the others that he was stronger than the rest.

I could hear some of the things being whispered about me. The whispers held a combination of awe, disdain, fear, hope and so many other emotions...all akin to water off a duck's back where I was concerned. What mattered was that they defeat me. Or rather, they did not, so that my little one's wish stood a slim chance of being fulfilled...

Amidst all the posturing, preening and pretending, a small group walked in, with dignity and grace. They were like a whiff of fresh air in an overcrowded and noisy market. Welcomed, seated, and then almost immediately ignored.

The contest commenced.

It took a while before the first one approached me. I suspect he was pushed towards me...

One after the other, they came. Big. Small. Old. Young. Brawny. Slim. Valiant. Vile. Foolish. Intelligent. Each eager to prove his might.

They pushed. And pulled. Huffed and puffed. Ranted and raved. They invoked their favourite Gods. Swore at one and all. Made fun of those who lost. And cursed me when they lost.

They climbed over me. Tried to get beneath me. They strained all their muscles. And put in all the strength they could muster, plus a little extra too.

All in vain though. Not one could move me by even a whisker.

A determination that my princess should get her heart's desire may have probably made me a little stronger – that is no compromise of my integrity, is it? It is just a deep-set desire, nay, prayer, of a father figure for the wellbeing of his little one.

.

A sense of despair filled the place. Those who had lost were plotting a combined attack. My host was thinking about what would happen, while my little one...

The look on her face was one of peace! And conviction. Even as I wondered about the serenity in her, I saw a bearded man nod to a young lad standing next to him.

.

With not a word said, the strapping lad came up to me, joined his arms in reverence, and bowed his head, as if seeking my permission to go ahead. Stretching out his hand, he grasped me at the middle. And lifted me up effortlessly!

Never had I felt so light. Or so blessed. His touch was... Magic. Divine. Loving.

A voice from another world seemed to whisper: "*This is why you were created. For this moment. And this moment alone. To bring together, in the eyes of this world, two beings who appear to be unrelated at this point of time.*"

As I was marvelling thus at his touch, he brought me down with a smooth movement, parallel to his body. Resting one foot on me, he raised his hand over his head with the intention of binding me at both ends.

And I surrendered to him.

Those who witnessed my surrender, and many after that, would say, "*The bow of the Destroyer was destroyed in the hands of the one who preserves.*"

Little do they realize that I was not destroyed. In my hurry to touch his feet, I merely bowed down. And deconstructed myself. For here I am, in your mind, narrating this momentous event. Reliving it. Revelling in it. Rejoicing in it.

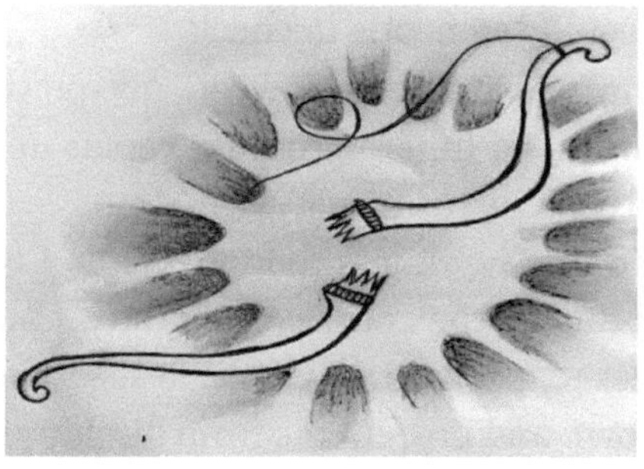

Shiva Dhanush

X

The Crossing

I am lethal.

Slim and curvaceous, a mere touch of mine can singe most. And if anyone tries to pit their strength against me, or attempts to cross me, they are bound to meet a painful end.

My strength lies in the fact that very few know of my existence.

I am very proud of myself. And why should I not be? I have, after all, been assigned a very important task - the mission of keeping someone in check.

It is going to be a test between my power and that person's feelings - of inherent nature versus upbringing, of clarity of purpose versus naivety.

I have one tiny weakness though. While I can fight the entire world during the course of my duty, I am powerless when it comes to a couple of people. Respect towards them will tie me down and prevent me from discharging my duty.

If I fail, a big IF, it will be because of one of them. Therefore, all I can hope is that the concerned person will not interfere with the scheme of things. As long as the said person does not take matters into their hands, I will be able to carry out my duty effectively. Call me a coward if you please, but I firmly believe that foolhardiness is not bravery, and it is always better to be safe than sorry.

.

I stand guard, vigilant. Watchful. Alert. Waiting for something to happen while hoping that nothing untoward will.

There is stillness in the air around me. Almost no noise – neither of the trees nor of any of the beings nearby or far away.

The atmosphere appears peaceful. The only sounds audible are those associated with a household. The lady of the house nearby is going about her routine chores while waiting for her family members to return.

She pretends to ignore me but is not indifferent to my presence. I, on my part, am happy as long as she does not come near me. Her stubbornness is something I do not want to deal with right now. It is best left to her family members.

.

A squirrel, probably unaware of my presence scampers towards where I am. It stops at the last second, just before colliding into me. Curious, it looks at me. A mere glare from me and it turns tail and scurries away. A few seconds later, I can hear its excited chatter. It is probably letting the others know about my existence while also warning them to keep away from me.

Within moments, I hear the birds and animals nearby chattering. Some of them, a handful of brave but foolish ones, dare to come close to me to get a better look. Not wanting to hurt them, and at the same time with the intention of warning them away, I start to lift my weapon.

They disappear in the blink of an eye, almost as if they have seen a ferocious demon and cannot wait to get away.

It appears as if my presence is no longer a secret. It does not bother me though. Come to think of it, the more others know about me, the easier it would be for me to perform my task well.

The birds and animals continue their excited chatter. Everything seems to be fine and under control. I relax.

.

The sudden cessation of sound shakes me out of my near stupor. The very next second, it is as if the calm has been broken in a placid lake due to a petulant child throwing a stone into its deep waters. The birds and animals nearby scatter away.

I look up to find a handsome mendicant approaching the place I am stationed at. Well built, he has the arrogance of a person who has gotten everything he has thirsted after.

He stops a little away from me and looks at his goal. Wonder, lust, and finally determination follow each other as the expressions on his face change rapidly. Quickly, in the blink of an eye, he masks his emotions and adopts a serene demeanour.

As he draws closer, I cannot but help admire his bearing and grace. I also see that he is clear about his goal, and determined to succeed.

.

But so am I. Determined to ensure that he fails, for that is my only job.

.

I am so slim that I am hardly visible. Unaware of my presence and power, he attempts to get past me, and I strike.

More astonished then hurt, he falls on his back. Getting up, and brushing aside the dust, he again tries to go past me.

I strike again. Another attempt and another failure.

Bewildered, he looks at the place where he was attacked and finally becomes aware of my presence.

A smart person, he realizes that if he were to come near me again, he will have to face my ire.

.

The perplexed look on his face makes me smile with glee. I sparkle.

I am enjoying this task. The battle is between my inherent nature and his. My sphere of influence versus his world of fear and control. My commitment versus his determination.

.

But alas, that is where I falter.

.

His determination is so strong that he resorts to devious means to get what he wants. And restricted that I am, I am not able to counter this cunning move of his.

He calls out to the lady of the house, demanding alms and provoking her to step beyond me. He does so by invoking the fame of her husband's family and their lineage.

Of royal blood that she is, and as one committed to traditional practices in addition to being married into a family that is known to give when asked, the lady unwitting, and with great reluctance does as told.

With alms in her arms, she steps over me, and respectfully goes up to the man who has been masquerading as a hermit till now. I cannot even cry out or warn her. I have no voice.

In a state of utter helplessness, I watch her walk away from me. And much as I want, there is nothing I can do to stop her, for she is one of the few people who can cross me and not be burned.

.

A shape shifter, even as she nears him, the cunning being assumes his actual form, that of the mighty ruler of the island nation down south, and whisks her away. His goal achieved.

.

And here I lie, helpless and having failed in the one task allocated to me - of protecting her. I remain there, waiting for my creator and his brother to return to an empty house.

.

One day, eons later, I will become synonymous with limits and boundaries of the moral kind. But today, all I am is a line drawn in dirt.

And a failure...

.

.

.

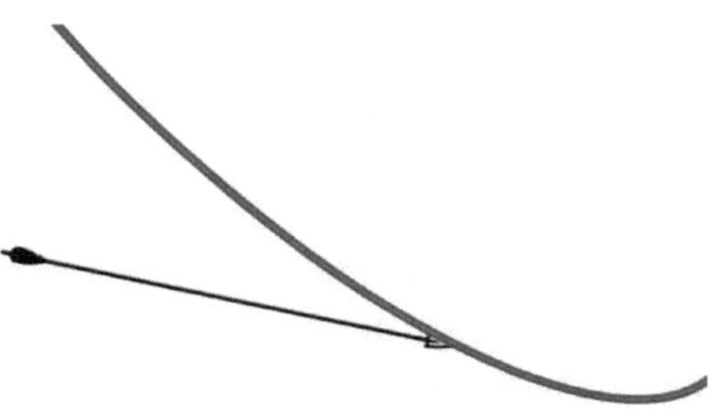

Lakshmana Rekhe

XI
The Indicator

I am hanging on.

Just barely though. For, if I let go, my master will most definitely die.

Both of us are being mercilessly pounded. We are covered in blood and bruises - blood that is starting to flow like a mini rivulet. I can't even begin to describe the pain of the battery we have been receiving. Suffice to say, it is the feeling of having been caught in the middle of a stampede with no way out.

The pain is blinding. My master is screaming in pain, and frustration too.

He has been putting up a worthy fight. But his opponent is so many times stronger – not just in body but in resolve too.

My master is a fugitive while his opponent is a ruler. My master has been subsisting for a long time on roots and wild fruits while his opponent has been enjoying all possible pleasures. My master believes that he is innocent of the crimes he has been charged with, while his opponent is certain that my master is guilty of them.

Love and respect have now degenerated into a bitter battle, a battle in which one of them has to die. And my master is hoping that it will not be him. That seems to be a near impossibility though. Any onlooker can see that my master and I are fast approaching a stage where we cannot hold on for much longer.

If there were onlookers, that is. I am starting to wonder if there is anyone nearby.

The forest, where this battle is taking place, has gone silent, except for my master's moans of pain, and his opponent's victorious cries every time he draws blood.

Not a leaf is stirring. Not an animal or bird in sight. The usually present motley crowd of apes and monkeys too seem to have dispersed, fearing that they may become unwilling targets in this battle.

What is worrying me though is that I am not able to spot the man who promised to help my master win this battle.

Has he too run away?

Has he realised how futile the situation is?

Has he decided that he would rather escape from the certain wrath of my master's opponent than face him?

While disappointed, I am not surprised. You would not be too if you were the recipient of the fast, furious and frequent poundings that my master and I are receiving. Blows are being rained on us like hail stones. Big, fat, bruising ones. We are being pinned to the trees, and to the rocks, and to the ground. And to every possible surface available.

Each time though my master is finding a way to escape. For how much longer though is a question I do not even want to think about.

My master is nearing the end of his strength. I can feel it even as I desperately try to hang on to him by a mere thread. I sense that he is about to give up and flee. If he can, that is. Or, should I say, if he is allowed to?

.

As we are being whirled around like a top, I catch sight of someone behind the trees. It is all a blur, for, the very next instant we are facing the other direction. And then another...

.

I hear a sharp whizzing noise .

And then a loud roar.

The roar is from my master's opponent. But there is something different in it this time. There is ... pain?!?

.

Even as I watch, the opponent slackens his hold on my master and falls to the ground. The arrow that struck him is causing him to bleed profusely.

As my master watches in relief, the person who shot the arrow comes over to where we all are. A conversation ensues between the shooter and the shot.

.

The scene being played out in front of me is strange, and sad too.

.

I see two pairs of brothers. But the similarity ends there. While there is complete love and respect between one pair, there is hatred and fear between the other. While one set of two brothers are considered the epitome of brotherly love, the other set will forever be remembered as sworn enemies. My master, unfortunately, belongs to the latter.

As I watch, my master's brother breathes his last. He does so after being promised by his killer that he will get a chance for revenge during a subsequent birth.

I am now drenched in the tears of my master. Tears of sorrow and regret, futile that they are.

Do I have any regrets? I would say 'No' for it was my job to protect my master. Or at least, be an indicator that would ensure that my master did not get shot at by mistake.

.

I have done by job well. I hung on to him when it was most needed. And because of that, my master will be able to help the shooter get back his wife from the clutches of the ten-headed one.

.

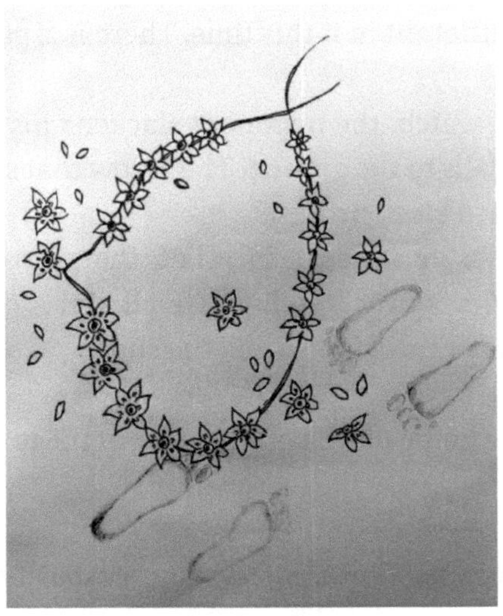

XII

The Wait

I am very lonely.

There are people all around me. All the time. And yet I feel lonely. Bereft. Burdened...

The reason: I have been separated, for over a decade now, from the one person I always wanted to be with.

No one asked me what my wish was in the matter. In fact, those involved in this act of separation did not care about my feelings. The result? I have been doing something that I would never have, had I had a choice.

Due to that one act of, may I call it, 'selfishness on the part of one person', from being a fellow traveller, I have been reduced to a position akin to a caged bird that is eternally on display.

•

Very often, I think that the one person I love and respect more than anyone else, sacrificed me on the altar of his affection. And he did so without considering my feelings even for a second...

At times, I have wondered if I am being punished for being proud that he initially chose me to accompany him on his journey. Maybe he wanted to remind me of my place...

There have been times when I have wanted to walk away from it all, especially when I have been feeling low. But then, I remember the great responsibility that has been placed on me by the one I respect, and I stay back.

•

The responsibility I shoulder was never an explicitly stated one. But the very fact that he sent me away from him is a clear message to me about what my prime responsibility is till the time I am reclaimed.

It is a burden I bear even as I wait and hope to soon bear a burden of another sort. A burden that would be the most lovable one, and that which most others would never get the opportunity to bear, ever.

In the meantime though, I fulfil the role assigned to me, silently and dutifully.

All the adulation and respect that has been shown to me all these years has not lessened my desire to be united with the person I value the most. The only consolation I have is that, by my presence here these past few years, I have been providing hope and direction to many, even though that is not what I wanted to do in the first place.

•

By the way, there are a couple of others who, like me, are doing things - you could call them duties - that they did not want to do. What is common among us is that we have all been doing it out of love and respect for the one whose return we await.

•

These past couple of days have been very difficult for all of us.

Just as the last mile appears to be the longest mile (who can know that better than me?), the wait has been highly unbearable. With no clear news, we are all desperately battling despair with hope.

.

Housed where I am, away from most people, I am feeling lonelier than ever. There is no one I can voice my worry to. In fact, there is no one who can understand my agony. Except perhaps the one who bears me. We have never talked about it though. And yet, our pain is similar.

I have an added worry today, a very large one, because, the person I was sent with all those years ago, is going to end his life in a few hours if the condition he had stipulated when I was passed on to his care is not be fulfilled. And the fact that I cannot do anything to stop him is steadily eating away at me.

I am in two minds about this person. On the one hand, I despise him for having taken me away from the one I wanted to be with always. And yet, I love him because he is loved by the one I respect. I am as such bound – I cannot walk away.

Right now, I am all alone. Waiting. Hoping. Praying... Just as everyone else has been doing these past few days.

.

Wait... what is it that I hear?

.

A distant shout.

A resounding cheer.

A glimmer of light. And hope...

.

I wait. Eagerly.

The cheers are growing louder by the second! The glow of light is drawing closer!! My anticipation is growing by the second.

The doors are thrown open. Light spills into the big, empty hall where I have been waiting impatiently all this while.

Countless lamps, joyous people and teary family members fill the hall. The sounds of welcome and cheer resound to the rafters.

.

And I wait. With bated breath.

.

The one I have been longing to be with all these years has finally returned. To claim his rightful place – the place that I occupy at this moment.

If I could, I would be dancing with joy. But all I can do is wait.

.

I can see him now. Finally!

.

He is coming towards me.

.

His face is calm. His bearing majestic. His walk graceful.

.

My wait is about to end!

.

His brother, the one I had been sent away with, bows to me in reverence and picks me up with care. Very lovingly, he places me at the feet of my master. The very feet I was separated from fourteen years ago.

.

My master dons me...

.

And my wait is finally over. I am back where I belong. At his feet. Serving him...

.

.

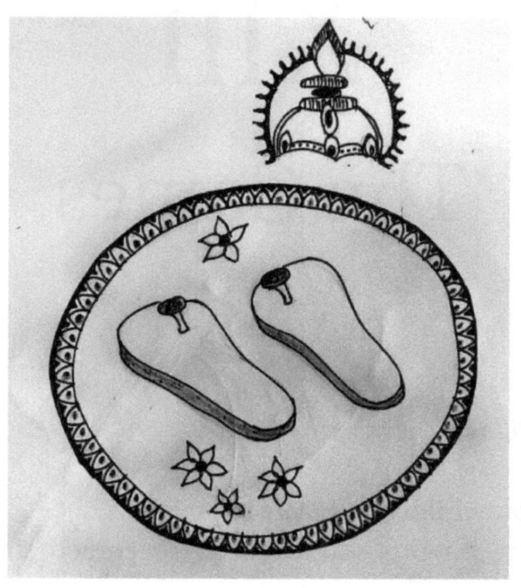

Rama Paaduka

XIII
The Games

The Villagers' perspective

"Are our children not safe anymore?"

Strange events have been reported from the neighbourhood these past few months. People and nature seem to be behaving in an extremely strange manner.

Like faithful soldiers in an extremely well choreographed sinister conspiracy, both man and nature seem to have turned against our children. So too have animals and inanimate objects!

The most recent incident reported is that of a person who was trying to lure away our young ones, especially those who were not even in their teens. He had managed to get them all together into a nearby cave. However, before much damage could be done, he died a mysterious death. His entire body bore bruises – clear signs of his having been battered to the ground countless times. But who did it remains a mystery!

A quick glance at the worrying events of the past:

A horse went on a rampage, almost biting off the fist of a boy.

A bull went berserk. Children and pregnant women nearby managed to escape with just a few scratches.

Earlier, a person masquerading as one of the locals attempted to kidnap a little boy. The same boy had been attacked by a donkey a few days ago!

A snake of humongous proportions was killed very close to the play area of our little ones before that.

A giant bird attacked one of our children a couple of days before the snake was discovered.

A shocking incident occurred when a calf, one of the gentlest creatures, attacked a child. This very child had, a few years ago, been blown a far distance away by a rouge whirlwind.

The child, in its infancy, had survived being crushed under a cart which broke down to pieces all of a sudden. This event had occurred a few months after the child escaped an attempt by a lady to poison him when he was barely a few days old!

Worrying indeed! Wonder what it would be next. Mad elephants???

The Mastermind's Instructions

"O evil beauty! Poison the little one's milk."

"O shape shifter. Crush the baby with your wood."

"You, twisted one. Blow the child away!"

"You, the not-docile one. Lure the child away with your innocent eyes & kill it."

"O the one with the beak like mouth. Peck the lucky child to death."

"You creepy & slimy one. Avenge the deaths of your silly sister and bird-brained brother. Kill that child!'

"You Ass! Destroy the child or, at least his brother!"

"You dumb-headed herdsman. Kill the older brother. The younger one will follow."

"O bull-headed one. Gore the child to death."

"O one with the lustrous mane. Trample the boy to death!"

"The one who can roam the skies. Kill all children. Not one should be spared!"

The Perpetrators' thoughts

"**I** am the best! **I** am the one who will please the Master. **I** will kill the child."

.

.

.

"What is happening??? How come I am failing?"

.

.

.

"I am finally free. For ever..."

ᘓ

The Child
This is fun!

ᘓ

Footnote:

The Mastermind is Kamsa.

The perpetrators, in the order of instructions given by Kamsa are:

1. Puthani - her breasts had poisoned milk
2. Shakata - a wooden cart
3. Trunavarta - a whirlwind
4. Vatsasura - a demon in the form of a calf
5. Bakasura - a huge crane (bird)

6. Aghasura - a large snake
7. Dhenukasura - a donkey that attacked Balarama
8. Pralamba - a demon in the form of a cowherd who tried to kidnap Balarama
9. Arishtasura - a bull
10. Keshi - a horse
11. Vyomasura - a demon who flew in the skies

And of course, the child is Krishna.

XIV
The Release

It all ended with a tug.

•

I am old and weighed down by my responsibilities. Therefore, if I forget some part of this tale, do fill the gaps using your imagination. And if I add to it, take it with a pinch of salt, as the ramblings of an old one.

•

Ever since I can remember, I and my ilk have been aiding the ladies of the village in their cooking. Be it a savoury dish or a special sweet, they have sought our help countless times.

Young ones, new brides, expectant mothers, watchful mothers-in-law, doting grandmothers – all of them have come to me at one time or other. Together, my friends and I have been, in general, making life easier for them for decades now, maybe centuries too.

•

Today is no different. As usual, we have been put to work since morning. As we go about our work, the little ones in the house too are going about theirs – overturning almost every vessel or thing within their reach, putting into their tiny mouths anything that they can lay their grubby little hands on, and, in general, making it near-impossible for the women to work.

.

The darling of the house is, in particular, so naughty that his mother is finding it very difficult to control the rambunctious one.

In exasperation, and as a last resort, she places the child in my care. Not one to be easily controlled, he keeps trying to slip away. With great determination, and I am sure with some divine intervention, she finally gets him to stay with me.

Heaving a sigh of relief, and with a glimmer of hope that she will get her work completed with minimum disturbance now, she turns and moves away towards the inner chambers of the house.

As she walks away without a backward glance, I can feel the little one's sobs raking his entire body. He strains to go after her but is restrained by me.

For a split second, I feel sorry for him. But that emotion lasts only for a second or two – for the duration it takes for him to turn and look at me with a totally bewitching smile. Something in me melts – and I am supposed to have a heart of stone.

.

I still wonder how I missed the mischievous glint in his eyes though...

The quick movement causes him to lose his balance, and the little one sits down with a slight thud. The unexpected accompanying pain, slight though it is, causes him to pucker his lips in a sob.

In anticipation, he looks around, but does not find his mother anywhere nearby. The pucker turns into a pout once her realises that he does not have an audience to cry to – I am of no consequence, for he knows that I shall pay him no heed. After a second glance round the place, almost automatically, the right thumb goes into his mouth and the baby lips close around it.

He finally rests against me, content for the time being. A gentle breeze wafts by, lulling the baby to sleep. As his eyes droop, I breathe a sigh of relief.

.

In haste, I realize the very next second, for a scampering squirrel wakes him from his state of near-slumber. Wagging its bushy tail, it looks at the boy, as if daring him to follow it. And can our little one refuse such a challenge? So, off he goes behind the squirrel, dragging me along with him. I try my best to hold him back, but he is unstoppable. He just keeps toddling forward, pulling me along with him.

Into the garden we go. And such a beautiful place it is. Full of fragrant flowers and wonderful plants. And trees!

It is near those trees that our little one last saw the squirrel. And he has to find it.

Determined, he rushes towards the trees. I think he spots something a little beyond the trees which catch his interest. So he sets off again, crawling through the barely-there space between two tall, old and dull trees.

He manages to get through. But I cannot, given my size. So what does he do? Pull me, of course!

.

And one sharp tug is all it takes...

.

To free the sons of the god of wealth from their curse.

.

With a resounding crash accompanying the fall of the trees, two radiant beings emerge from the now-fallen-trees, fold their hands in gratitude, and rise towards the heavens.

And the child sits there with an innocent smile on his face...waiting for his parents to come and kiss him, and pamper him. Yet again.

What about me?

Well, I have waited just long enough to narrate this tale to you. I too am on my way heavenwards – if you were to ever seek me, all you will probably find is a lifeless stone.

XV

The Cleansing

I am cursed.

•

I was, not very long ago, loved and respected by all around me.

People would flock to me. So important did they consider me that they would, without fail, include me in all their festivities. Some had even composed songs in my praise. I was happy, and so were those with and around me.

Until the day the boundaries I had set were crossed, one can say violated, without my permission.

I was caught unaware. Unprepared. Helpless to defend myself.

My welcoming nature had become my curse and there was nothing I could do about it. Not then. And not to this day.

•

The perpetrator continues to take advantage of my nature. What is saddening is that even those who depend on me are not being spared. Their mere association with me has inevitably resulted in unforeseen and grievous consequences.

Today, I am no longer revered. People avoid me whenever possible. I am no longer welcomed into their homes. In fact, they make it a point to specifically instruct every newcomer or visitor to avoid me.

I watch them pass by – hoping they will look at me, and maybe come near me. But then again, I consciously will them away, as far away as possible, for I know that they will have to pay a heavy prize if they come anywhere near me.

But somehow, this day, ***today***, seems to be different.

The sun has cast a warm glow all around, and the birds are chirping joyously. There is a fragrant wafting about. Every now and then, the trees nearby are showering a couple of flowers on me. I am filled with an inexplicable hope...

I spot a small boy coming this way, a spring in each step of his. Will he come closer, I wonder. Or like all others, will he turn away from my now lacklustre and poisoned body?

He is drawing closer. Oh! What a bewitching smile! And such beauty. I wish I could just touch and caress him for a moment...

His touch! It is so gentle and soothing. Filled with love.

Can he see my tears of joy? Dare I reach up and draw him into my folds?

No. No. NO! I cannot risk having him being attacked by my violator. It is best that I pull away from him right this moment before he is spotted.

I can feel the loss of his touch. Oh, I have never lamented my fate like I am now.

The boy too must have remembered what his elders have been telling one and all. He has turned his back to me and is walking away.

He has stopped. At the rock nearby. But why? Oh, to tighten the cloth around his waist – little one, it must have come lose when he bent towards me.

He has turned towards me... He looks like a little warrior standing there, with his hands planted firmly on his waist. The sun has formed a golden halo around his head. I can sense the little one's smile though I cannot see it.

What is he doing??? Why is he coming near me again?

There, a little distance away, I can see his friends and loved ones running towards him. Gesticulating, shouting something. The tumultuous wind is blowing away most of what they are saying. But do I hear "...na... stop... dangerous ..."?

Why do I feel this sudden tingling sensation? The warmth... The peace! The relief. It is heavenly. As if a dewdrop has kissed the Chataka bird...

The din caused by all those people standing nearby is unbearable. The crying out. The sobbing in anguish. The fear. The helplessness. "He jumped! ... will be killed... without him, we will die..."

Oh. How could I forget about the little boy? So selfish have I become that I am not thinking of his safety at all.

Their lament is causing grief to me too. For after all, it was with me that the boy was seen last... I will now be branded forever as the one who caused the death of a much-loved child.

My grief and tears can be seen by none – they do not matter anyway.

Wait. What is that I hear? A lone clear voice. Of another young boy – the brother of the first. Saying, “Don’t worry! He will be fine.”

What is this that I am experiencing? Something fluttering on my bosom? The warmth of a lamp in a dark cave. A waft of fresh air being let into a room that had been closed for ages.

I can sense the violent rage of the vile one. And his utter disbelief as he is held and mercilessly tossed about like a limp rag.

I can feel the invisible shackles that had bound me all these days melt away.

I can sense HIS fear and my liberation.

Tiny feet that pitter patter around the village, bringing joy to all its inhabitants, are now stomping to a totally separate and intense tune.

On him. And each time he tries to look up, he is ruthlessly pushed down by those stubby legs.

I swell with joy and raise my arms to the sky for those gathered near me to behold...

“There he is! Our little one! Alive. And dancing away to glory on the multiple hoods of that dreaded snake!!!”

“Look at his grace. And the ease with which he is controlling the dark one. Blessed are we indeed to witness this divine dance. Hail, oh dusky one!”

Cleansed am I now.

And blessed. For I became the watery stage on which the omnipresent, in the form of a tiny tot, danced the dance of victory over evil.

And now, I flow on. Free. Pure.

And once again, revered by countless people.

The river Yamuna

XVI

The Shower

"Attack!"

That thunderous order would have sent shivers down the spine of most seasoned warriors. And you are after all just a fledging, still wet behind the ears...

Drawing on all the courage you can muster, and with the thrill of being drafted in your first battle ever, you rush forward.

Were it a few days ago, you would not have been allowed anywhere near the warriors who are an elite and highly respected group.

As was the practice in other lands, children and youngsters were rarely allowed near such a group of highly trained soldiers. At best, you would have been considered extremely lucky if you were to catch a glimpse of some of them, from afar, as they took off to distant lands.

You alone will know how many times you have sneaked away from the protective fold of your elders to watch, in stealth, and with some amount of envy, these proud warriors train even as you hope that, one day, you too would be a part of this powerful group.

Loved and protected by your elders, you have, until this moment, not been given anything serious or important to do. Yet today, you have been summoned because the prestige of your leader, and as a direct consequence, your entire clan, is at stake.

.

A motley group of villagers have dared to violate a sacred pact! A pact they had entered into with your forefathers decades ago. Years of relationship has broken by one thoughtless decision, and the action of a few elders of that village, who, after this senseless act, can only be considered senile.

They and their people will now have to pay for this gross violation! And you will be a part of that team which will bring them to their knees.

.

Despite being young and uninitiated, you have the advantage of having travelled into enemy territory before today. You therefore know the lay of the land. Remember? A year ago, when the treaty was still in place and was being honoured, you had accompanied your father, an ambassador, on one of his tours. At that time you had marvelled at the simplicity of the villagers and the love they showered on their young ones.

You had, in fact, been very tempted to join a group of exuberant youngsters playing at the banks of the river. But sadly, protocol had demanded that you do not mix with them. You had, as such, very reluctantly, and with no small amount of envy, watched them from afar: chasing after each other, playing pranks on their elders, and yet, getting away with nary a punishment each time. You can, to this day, remember the joy and laughter penetrating through the air around that village.

And yet, here you are today, waging war on the very people you had envied a few months ago. All because of a decision taken by a leader who considers himself custodian of all things '*right*'.

Strange indeed are the ways of life.

.

Today is the seventh day of the war. And the first day that you have been drafted. It appears as if your commanders have grossly underestimated the resilience of the villagers. News has been trickling down the ranks that a show of strength from your side, which should have had the desired effect in a few hours, has now turned into a do-or-die situation. There is anger, frustration and despair throughout the camp.

The strength and supplies of the entire force have been depleted to a very sorry state. Warriors who would earlier show off their prowess have returned home drained and defeated. The most powerful weapons in the arsenal have had no effect – it is as if they have all been deflected by an impregnable shield protecting the villagers.

Dire situations call for dire actions. Your leader has no choice left – he must either send a team of greenhorns into the battlefield, or surrender. He, and you, do not want the latter. So, here you are, rushing towards enemy territory, along with your friends, dressed in your spiffy uniform of blue, grey and silver, with your weapon of choice gleaming in the sunlight.

.

As you near the village, a strange sight meets your eyes. The village is empty – not a soul to be seen. The commander of your platoon points towards a range of hills nearby and says, "They are hiding there. We need to flush them out.

Forward March!"

As your unit rushes towards the hills, you quietly sneak away. A very strong thought is tugging at you, saying, "*Attack from within.*" Also in you is the strong desire to prove to your people that you can help win an important war. For, if you could turn the tide of this war today, you will forever be known as the valiant one who successfully did what the best of best had failed to do. Name and fame would be yours.

Stealthily, you creep up to the place where the villagers have taken shelter, wanting to see if you can infiltrate the group and get to their leader. You are also curious to know what prompted them to shift allegiance from your powerful leader to a mere sedentary piece of rock.

•

All you can see are people, people and more people. Young and old. Men and women. Infirm and healthy. And with them, all the cattle of the land. The most amazing thing though is that there is not a sign of fear or worry on a single face!

Peacocks are dancing to the song of the birds. Babies are crawling about. Children have gathered around grandparents to listen to tales from the past. Men are milking the cows and feeding them, while women are preparing the food. Each one is smiling and going about their work as if it were just any other day.

That it has been incessantly raining this past week, as a result of which they have been driven away from their homes seems to have no effect on them at all! There is only love and laughter under this single huge shelter.

•

Clinging to the hill, you move towards the middle of the group where you are sure you will find their leader. And what do you see? A young boy, standing casually, with his left hand touching the hill. You approach him from behind. Wanting to catch him by surprise.

.

On the contrary, you are caught unawares.

.

As if sensing your presence, the boy turns around. And smiles at you. And you halt in your tracks. Mesmerized. Stunned. Bewitched by his dusky beauty.

.

And then, it dawns on you what it is that you need to do. With reverence, you go down to him, and adoringly, after having unknowingly waited for a year, caress his dark face, gently stroke the little finger that is so easily, and playfully, holding up the huge hill, and touch his feet in ardent worship.

Realizing that the purpose you were created for is going to be fulfilled at this moment, you lovingly wash his dainty feet with all the water stored in you.

.

A while later, your leader, accompanied by others, will come to seek pardon of this divine cowherd. And give him a new name – the protector of cows. But right now, this moment, is just between the dark hued one and you – he is showering on you his grace just as you have showered on him everything that you had.

The purpose of your life has been served. Blissfully, you float away...

.

XVII

The Lovers

I love her!

And as long as there is breathe in me, I will love her.

.

Yet, we are destined to part.

.

It would be impossible to find lovers like us. Ask this earth who has borne countless beings or the wind that blows all over – both will agree with what I say.

Our love will never be understood for we were never meant to be together in the first place. Destiny however had other plans and we were thrown together...

We have since witnessed and been part of the greatest love story of all times. We in fact met because of them...

.

They – the most captivating couple ever known.

She – fair, slender, radiant, innocent and deeply in love with him.

He – dark, handsome, bewitching, mischievous and so very in love with her.

.

Stories, poems and songs will be composed about their love – now and forever – so pure and real is it. And so timeless.

Many will yearn to have love like theirs. Others will envy it. And yet, no one will ever love like them...

•

She yearns to spend all her time with her while he pines away for her. So in love with him is she that she has broken many rules specified by society. So in love with her is he that he has eyes for no other.

When they are away from each other, the world appears colourless and meaningless to both. And when they are together, the world disappears. There is no one else, nothing else.

So tender and beautiful is their love that it brings tears to the eyes of those who happen to witness their stolen moments of togetherness. That is us, most times.

Each is completely immersed in the love of the other. They are like one soul in two bodies. And their love is so pure, it hurts.

All she wishes for is his presence. And he... he wants to hold her in his arms and keep her there forever.

•

The biggest tragedy of all times is that their love will never culminate in marriage. Ever. They are destined to part.

They know it. And that is what makes their love even more precious. More beautiful. More poignant.

They are meeting for the last time tonight. As are we...

•

We were thrown together when they started meeting. And very soon, we became an excuse, a reason, for them to meet! But when they met, they would completely forget us.

So much in love were they.

It was not long before their love rubbed off us. We were after all silent accomplices in their trysts, accompanying them each time. Gradually, our love too blossomed.

There is hardly anything common between us. I am slim and tall while she is round and short. I am more used to giving while she is best at holding. I am light hearted while she is large hearted.

Come to think about it, there are some similarities too. Both of us love our friends and are their constant companions. We both love music. And we are both fixed in our ways.

No one will ever talk about our love. No one knows about it. Our friends are so in love with each other that they have never observed our love. Or maybe they have... we do not know. And will never know. For today is our last day together...

Today... tonight... now...

He is holding her to him, wiping her tears while barely keeping his at bay.

Neither is saying a word, so choked with emotions are they. The moment of separation is fast approaching...

Filled with love, tenderness and angst, he bends down, lovingly caresses her feet, and reverently places them on his head before she can even realize what he is up to.

With love overflowing in her eyes mingling with tears, she hurriedly tries to pull her feet away. She considers it sacrilege that her feet should even touch his head. But the divine lover that he is, he holds on to her feet. Unabashedly allowing his tears to wash them.

She reaches out with a trembling hand and touches his lovely face...

Both of us turn away. These last few moments of their togetherness are too private to be a witness to. And most painful.

As for us, we cannot cry. We cannot even hold each other. All we can do is pray...

Krishna's flute and Radha's pot

XVIII

The Avowal

He was young and handsome!

The radiance in his face caught the eye of women and men alike, as did his iron-hard muscles and height.

Admiration and envy were the common reactions evoked when one set eyes on him. The women admired him, while the men – well – there was a tinge of envy in their admiration.

Seated comfortably on a white horse that appeared to be flying, he looked magnificent.

He was the son of a committed mother and a capable father. And it showed. At a very young age, his mother had ensured that he was tutored by the best of the best, be it in political science, archery or the sacred texts. From his father he had learnt the art of administration. That he excelled in each and every area was not a surprise, given his commitment to learning.

Not only was he admired for his mental dexterity, his physical prowess too was without any doubt. His valour was the topic of many a conversation. He was now of an age where parents of young girls secretly hoped that he would become their son-in-law.

He had in fact, just this morning, had a conversation with a well-wisher about adding another member to his family. Through holy matrimony, of course.

The damsel in question was... Beautiful. Exquisite. Charming. Her innocence was bewitching. When she was nearby, it was as if she brought a waft of perfumed air with her – so captivating was she. An obedient daughter, she helped her father in his daily chores. Having learnt from a previous experience, she had left it to her father to decide who her husband would be.

.

It was with the steadfast intention of convincing her father that he had set out. He was very sure that his father would have no objection to the alliance. He knew that wooing her father would be an uphill task. But then he was also very confident about his capabilities. He was very clear that, before the day was out, he would have her father's consent.

.

Tethering his horse to a tree near the riverbank, he strode over to where her father sat. Bowing down to him in respect, he voiced his request in a clear and confident voice. Only to be told very curtly, "No!"

Unfazed, he sought clarification for the refusal. And the reason he was given made him do something so unexpected and so shocking that the entire world was shaken.

It was as if time stood still – in a vain attempt to capture that moment for posterity. Stunned onlookers could not contain their surprise. The damsel and her father were taken aback too, for this was definitely not the response they had expected, not even in their remotest dreams.

.

The earth shuddered – the pain of a mother was not new to her. The heavens shook. The river swelled up as if in an attempt to drown away his voice. Thunder and lightning accompanied his pledge, **"I, the son of Ganga, with the five elements and all the Gods and Goddesses as my witness, hereby declare that I shall never marry anyone. Ever."**

.

And thus was born one of the greatest legends ever. A man so true to his word that he was thereafter known by the oath he took. And the destiny of an entire dynasty was rewritten.

.

.

ꙮ

XIX
The Retrieval

'Hide and Seek' is my favourite game.

Do not be fooled by what others tell you. They have their own thoughts about what I am good for. I do concede that I am good at most of the things they attribute to me. Yet, given a choice, and at every possible opportunity, I indulge in playing hide and seek, with me being the one who is sought.

Today is no different. My friends and I have taken over a field away from the hustle and bustle of the capital.

We have been playing since morning. Flying across the glade, rushing down the slope, cutting across lush green fields -- it has been a wonderfully exhilarating day for me.

I am now tired. And want to rest. But my friends are showing no signs of taking a break. They are keen on continuing, competing with each other, chiding and provoking each other.

Split into two groups, each group member wants to prove that he is better than the other group's members. And that has been their aim since morning – in everything they have done.

I belong to neither group. And am now tired of their childish play. All I want to do is get away from them and rest for a while.

Ah! What is it that I see? The ideal spot for me to rest!

At the first possible opportunity, I fly to that spot. Finding myself a nice place to relax, I indulge in a refreshing swim too. The water is cold and the place cool. After a long exhausting day, I am finally alone and able to do what I have been wanting to do for a while now.

I can hear my friends searching for me. They are looking for me everywhere nearby, arguing with each other about where I may be.

Finally, one of them mentions that he saw me moving towards my current hiding place and they all converge near where I am.

They can see me but are not able to convince me to come out. They are not even able to find a way of coming close to where I am.

Or maybe, they are just lazy – they are probably looking for someone else to do what they should and could be doing, that is bring me out.

With a look of glee on my face, I watch them debating amongst themselves. How to get me out of my current 'hiding' place is the point of debate.

Right now, I am their most important player – they cannot continue playing without me. And they cannot find an immediate replacement either.

The fact that they are finding themselves helpless and incapable of getting me out of my hiding place is giving me great joy.

I roll around and kick back, enjoying my leisurely swim. My friends' attempts are making me smile – something I am doing after a very long time. I have been kicked about and hurled around by them enough number of times to warrant this break.

What is it that I see? And hear? My friends have turned away from me and are talking to someone.

And then, a shadow... Bigger than that of my friends.

The sun is shining down on all of us. Due to my current position, I am unable to make out who the newcomer is. He says something to my friends and they respond, explaining their current predicament.

All I hear is his voice as he draws closer to my hiding place. The voice... it is commanding. I can detect arrogance and confidence too. And just that tiny bit of contempt – enough to make my friends respond in a defensive manner.

"Let us see how you can help us retrieve..." the voice of one of the older brothers tapers off even as he makes the statement. While I do not know what has transpired just now between him and the newcomer, I can guess that the former must have been silenced by a condescending look by the latter.

Curious now, I look up. I can see the silhouettes of my friends and of a man, the newcomer, I presume. All of them are looking at me. I am too far for them to pull me towards them. As I watch, I see the newcomer lift a hand, and also hear him mutter something.

Ah! Something has pierced my skin!

.

A blade of grass. A blade of grass? A blade of grass!!!

.

Here comes another. And another. And another...

.

Even as I watch spellbound, within seconds the newcomer fashions a kind of stick, with each new blade of grass piercing and holding on to the previous blade.

Then, with great ease, I am pulled out. And held in the hand of the one who will be soon known as the greatest teacher ever.

Surrounding him are my 105 friends, brothers and cousins all, who will, within a very short time, become the students of this great man. And who will fight with and against him in the greatest war ever that will take place in their lifetime.

.

I will never learn from him. But I shall always be remembered as the one who brought about this meeting between a great guru and his disciples.

The ball being pulled out of the well by Dronacharya

XX
The Gift

I am bleeding. To death.

In a short while, all that will remain of me is my lifeless form. Therefore, give me your ear so that, before I am drained of life, I can narrate to you that which has come to pass.

We are five siblings. While I am usually a little aloof from the rest, I have the capacity to hold us together. And when that happens, we are a force to reckon with.

We, along with our cousins, have served our master from the time he was born. We have been an integral part of almost each and every aspect of his growth and life – right from the time he was a toddler who would reach out to the feathers adorning his father's headgear, to the time he started standing up and walking, and also when he held his implement of choice for the first time. And ever since.

Let me tell you something about our master. He is a very determined person. Once he makes up his mind about something, nothing can prevent him from accomplishing what he wants. He does everything that is necessary to get the result he desires. Nothing illegal or immoral, let me hasten to add.

Nothing has stopped him – neither rejection nor insult nor hidden agendas. On the other hand, such negative reactions have only strengthened his determination. We have been silent witness to this facet of his, and his willing companions in all his endeavours.

.

Our master's life these past few months has been one of practice. And more practice. From dawn to dusk. His daily routine has been the same - right from the time of his waking up to his offering salutations to his teacher to learning the use of, and practicing with his chosen armaments till much after the sun has set. Every day, without fail.

We have been witness to his skill improving – seen him grow from being a mere novice to becoming the best of the best. Needless to say, we have been with him, serving him faithfully the entire time. It would not be an exaggeration if we were to say that it is because of our help that he has become the expert that he today is. Well, was until a few minutes ago...

.

You think I am exaggerating about his ability because I

used to serve him? Well, sample this. Just a short while ago he successfully prevented a dog from barking – the dog which had been disturbing his practice. My master did not kill it or harm it in any manner. All he did was let fly a few arrows in a particular formation which effectively prevented the dog from closing its mouth - all without shedding a single drop of its blood.

.

But alas, this superior skill of his is what has resulted in me being separated from him. For ever.

.

Someone else saw this dog with the arrows in its mouth and came searching for my master. Someone who had witnessed such expertise before.

.

Who is it, you ask me? Well, none other than our master's teacher. The very same one to whose effigy our master respectfully bows down to every morning, even though the former did not accept him as a student. The very same one who our master has always considered his teacher – for he is indeed the greatest teachers of all times.

.

When asked who his teacher was, our master had pointed to the statue and very humbly responded that the one who had come searching for him, and was now asking him who his teacher was, was indeed his teacher.

And what did this 'great' teacher ask of our master in return?

Me!

.

I am sure our master was shocked by this response. Pained even. Hurt too. And yet, what did he do when he realised that his teacher was indeed very serious about the Gurudakshina he was seeking?

With a sad smile plying on his lips, our master took out his knife and, with nary a hesitation, brought it down on me.

Forever separating me from my siblings and himself.

And so I lie on the ground, watching everyone walking away from me. My master too – without a backward glance.

.

I am bleeding to death. Angry. And sad.

Angry not because my master sacrificed me, but because, by this selfless act of his, my master will no longer be known as the most powerful warrior of his times. I am sad not because I will not be able to serve my master again but because no one else can ever take my place. And because of this, my master will forever live with a handicap.

.

The consolation I have at this point of time, when the blood in me is nearly all drained away, and I am soon going to be the food of some scavenger is that, my master will be known for ever after, as the great student who gave his teacher the fees he demanded.

XXI

The Transgression

We are beautiful.

Slim and curvaceous, we are elegance personified. At the same time, there is nothing subtle about us. Naturally beautiful, we love being adorned with jewels.

We have been admired by many, and envied by many more. The reason is simple – not everyone has companions as beautiful as us.

We owe our allegiance to only one person. And with her we shall stay until our last breath. The lady and her people have taken excellent care of us from the time we remember. No ordinary care, mind you. We have been nurtured as one would a child, and pampered like one would a princess. On special occasions, we have been adorned with the most beautiful embellishments available, causing envy to many who are less fortunate.

We in turn have done our job to her utmost satisfaction – each time.

We have been very well protected too. Only a select few can come close to us, and these are mostly members of the lady's intimate circle. The rest can only admire us from afar.

We are also privy to some of her most important and intimate moments. The first time she saw her husband. The first time she met her mother-in-law. The first time she gave birth.... The bond that binds us to her is very strong.

.

Given the nature of our relationship, we take liberties with her that very few others can, be it covering her eyes, tickling her waist or caressing her cheeks. She chides us sometimes when we do so; but we know that she likes it too. And we do it only when we are free to do so.

.

Today is one such day.

.

All of us are in her inner chambers, enjoying a 'ladies-only' moment, with her and a few others. The topics discussed include husbands, families, relatives, travels, and the latest happenings. The speed with which the topics are changed is amazing – like a swift moving wind that changes direction at will. We try to keep pace, but give up after a while.

For the time being, we are happy to do nothing except rest. And play pranks on her once in a while.

.

A hefty man storms in all of a sudden. And the peace is shattered! He should not be here – not in these inner chambers of women. And yet he is. His menacing stance and ugly glare causes everyone's blood to run cold.

.

She stands up with a start. In her regal manner, she asks him to leave. He laughs. The mere sound of his foul laughter grates on our nerves.

She repeats her command. He only draws closer, the look on his face vile and orders her to accompany him. She refuses.

.

With glee, he catches hold of some of us and starts pulling us, forcing her to follow in the process. She tries to free us from his clutches – but his hold is too strong, maniacal even. Dragging us, he reaches his intended destination: a big hall overflowing with people, mostly of royal blood, and many of them family.

And then commences the most heinous act of outraging the modesty of a chaste woman. In the presence of one and all. Some of them taunt her. Insult her. Jeer at her. Make demeaning gestures. Pull at her clothes...

.

We try to shield her. In vain. We are so weak that we are not capable of protecting her. For the very first time, we feel very superficial and of little use. We are angered that we made it easy for someone to treat her thus. Our rage is however impotent.

.

She beseeches the elders assembled to save her. They look away. She argues with, and then implores her partners to do something. All but one sit with their heads bowed in shame. She reasons, cajoles, demands, chastises...to no avail.

.

In despair and as a last resort she calls out the one with whom she shares a name. And he, despite being far away from us all, saves her modesty in the blink of an eye.

.

As everyone watches this miracle, awestruck, the one who first tried saving her, the one who loves her the most, the one who is known for his immense strength, declares, "*I shall wash your hair with his blood – the very hair he had had the audacity to touch!*"

These words reverberate across the packed hall and send shivers down the spine of the perpetrator and his brothers. They pretend to laugh it off. But we know, as does everyone else, that their days are now numbered.

Our wait has just commenced. It will be thirteen years before our hurt and anger will be washed away by the blood of the second among a hundred...

XXII
The Satiation

I am unique.

No one else can do what I do so effortlessly. It is a fact that I have been quietly effective each time I have been pressed into service. And it is also a fact that I am proud about it.

What I can do in seconds takes even the best of best, hours to do. Believe me, I am not exaggerating when I say so.

I have delivered faultlessly – each and every time.

I enjoy my position of importance in the family I am currently with. Each of them respects me, and values my work. It would not be far from the truth if I were to say that they depend on me to a great extent.

Obtaining my services had not been easy. The head of the family had to pray to his grandfather in whose custody I was, before I was sent to be with them.

Efficient though I am, I am particular about one thing. While I am willing to work from dawn to dusk, once I am given a break from work during the day, I will get back to work only on the following day. That condition of mine has been accepted and respected by the family members. On my part, I ensure that, the lady of the house who takes care of me, is, in turn, taken care of by me each day.

All of us are happy with this agreement.

Today is no different. The sun is beaming down on us. The river nearby is reflecting its dazzling light. The chirping of birds can be heard, alongside the usual sounds of the household.

The family members are all getting ready to go about their business for the day. The lady of the house has been at work since morning – cleaning, feeding her family, and taking care of the routine chores. It is only now that she has been able to sit down and partake of her meal.

Satiated, and with a feeling of well being, the dark hued beauty sits back. She appears to be enjoying the solitude that has been temporarily granted to her.

Through her actions, she indicates that my job for the day is done. Content, and after a refreshing wash, I too settle down.

As I start to nod off, I hear voices. They appear to be coming from outside the window. The lady of the house too hears them and steps out to investigate.

From the sounds drifting towards me from outside, I glean that some unexpected visitors have dropped in to meet the family members. The latter are very good hosts. It is as such not surprising that people keep visiting them at will.

As I slip into a state of near slumber, I hear the lady say something to the effect, "... cannot help us now. What do we do?"

The worry in her voice is palpable. Something very important and urgent seems to be the matter. I wonder about it briefly but do not pay much head to it. I know that the lady is extremely capable and will do whatever is needed to get the result she desires.

.

Something breaks my reprieve – a sense of being stared at. I glance up to find the lady looking at me – her expression is a combination of worry, hope and resignation. The look is enough to tell me that something is wrong.

The look she gives me is beseeching and would have melted the heart of stone. I am however unable to do anything to help as I am completely drained.

Realizing that I will not be able to help her out of her current predicament, the lady turns and calls out to the one she considers her brother. And, in a flash, he appears before her.

Sensing her distress, he asks her the reason. Using very few words, she explains the challenge that her family members are facing.

.

The cause for her worry is indeed genuine, as one of the many guests who have come un-announced is known to be extremely short-tempered and harsh while also being powerful. The onus of taking care of his current demand rests totally on her shoulders.

.

The dark hued one listens to his sister's concerns, and ...smiles. With a twinkle in his eyes, he says, "*I am hungry.*

Feed me first. I be able to think about how we can deal with the others only after my hunger has been satiated."

Distressed, the lady stares at him with reproach and responds in a tone tinged with acquisition, "How could you be so heartless? Asking me for food! You know the problem - there is nothing left to eat right now! Not a bit!"

He smiles again and says, "Be frank and let me know if you do not want to feed me. Why lie?"

Enraged, the lady grabs me and thrusting me before him says, **"See! Nothing!"**

.

The one with the bewitching smile, the master of the universe, puts out a finger, the one that on occasions bears the divine discus, and touches me.

I shiver in ecstasy and joy.

And shudder in pain as I realize that I cannot offer him anything. For the first time I wish that I were not bound by the condition I operate under. Here, before me, stands the one who feeds the universe, and I am unable to bring up even one morsel of food for his consumption.

.

I, who till now was proud of my capacity to feed thousands within the blink of an eye lid, am of no use at this hour of need. My ego lies shattered at the feet of this great being.

Shamefaced, I try to slip away. But the bewitching one refuses to let go. He pulls out a morsel of food that had stuck to me till now – something that I and the lady had overlooked.

.

Another smile, a knowing one this time, and into his beautiful mouth goes that last morsel of food.

.

And down by the river, the angry one and his hundreds of companions suddenly realize that they are no longer hungry. They, on the other hand, experience the satiation of having partaken of and over-indulged in the most delicious and lavish spread ever. All they want to do now is find a place to nap.

Even as the family members watch in bemusement, the unexpected guests exit the place in seconds with a hurried 'Good bye'.

.

The family is saved from the wrath of the angry one.

.

And I...

.

I will be immortalized in stories. And for ever after, many will remember me while talking about abundance of food and all things good.

.

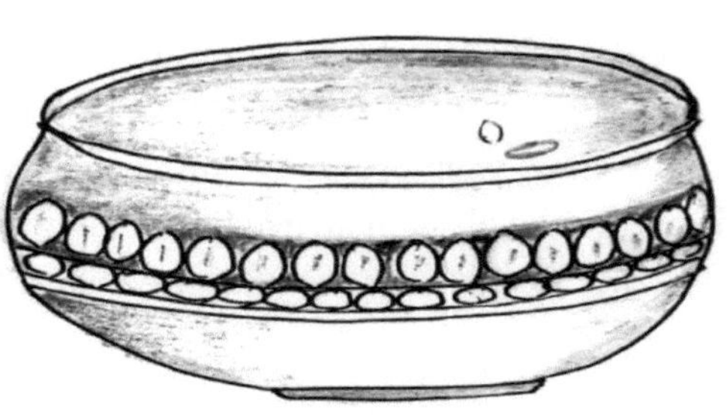

Akshaya Patre

XXIII
The Meeting

We had never seen him before.

His family members, yes. Him, never. At least not before today.

It was a glorious day when he came to us. The air had a fragrant smell to it, and the earth beneath our feet was soft and welcoming. The whole place around us seemed to vibrate with joy as if preparing for some momentous event.

Maybe we read too much into an act of nature. Maybe we expected too much. For, after all the beauty and wonder displayed by nature, who came to us? Someone who was small, old and frail... And what did he do? Just roll up and go to sleep!

It took us a while to get over our disappointment.

We had to offer our hospitality to him though – it was our bounden duty. But we did not care much about him. To give him credit, he too did not expect much in terms of hospitality from us. He seemed content with a fruit or two. Or maybe, he was just very tired – he had probably been travelling long distances for a while now.

Courtesy demanded that we neither abandon nor trouble him. As such, I remained with him while the rest continued doing what they had to do. I did not have to exert myself too much either, as he soon started slipping into a state of sleep.

.

At one point of time, he leaned on me. And, was it a coincidence? I wonder, for, at that exact same moment, I felt a cool breeze touch me. It was a wonderful feeling. I allowed myself to be caressed and cosseted by the wind – almost as if a father were pampering a favourite child.

.

Soon the sun started its ascent.

Our 'guest' would not have been able to bear the heat, let alone face the sun. I therefore ensured that he was fairly shielded from the powerful rays of the sun. I could not help but feel sorry for him as he continued to lie down, reluctant to move to a better place.

He seemed so much at peace – mumbling something in his sleep all the time – a soothing sort of mumble that caused my heart to mumble too - without realizing what I was doing.

.

Even as I was wondering whether or not to wake him up, I was distracted by a whiff of fragrant air. So aromatic was it that I was tempted to seek the source. A divine flower probably. My self-appointed duty prevented me from doing so. I however continued to enjoy the fragrance while also taking in the unusual peace and calm that seemed to have gently fallen all around as a soft blanket.

.

The sun's warmth, and the cool breeze together lulled us into a state of semi-sleep. The birds, animals, trees and plants all around us too seemed to be in a state of relaxation. Gradually, everyone nodded off.

.

The earth shook.

.

And before one could think of it as a one-off event, it shook again. And again. And again! The calm was shattered.

The birds shot out of their perches with a startled cry while many hatchlings fell off their nests. The animals scattered in all directions, running or slithering, hither and thither. The entire area was suddenly filled with the cacophony of birds and disoriented animals.

Rooted to our places, we waited in horror as the earth continued to shake. The tremors seemed to be getting closer and closer.

There was a steady rhythm to the tremors though - as if someone was running and stomping on the ground while doing so. As the quakes intensified and appeared to draw closer, periodic shouts akin to roars could also be heard.

Surprisingly, our guest was not disturbed by all this – he probably was in such deep sleep that he did not realize that his life could well be in danger.

The tremors grew closer. The roars louder. And soon we could see a cloud of dust in the distance. From that huge moving cloud on the ground kept appearing, almost rhythmically, uprooted trees of various sizes and varieties - all whizzing through the air like missiles.

From the very same cloud shot out disturbed and scared birds. Any animal that, by a cruel twist of fate, happened to have the misfortune of being in the way of that moving cloud, was quickly swallowed up by it and soon lost from sight. We did not even dare to think what could have happened to those unfortunate creatures.

As the cloud drew closer, I realized that we were in its way, and were very likely to meet a fate similar to the others.

.

A quick word here about the old one. In the past few minutes, unknown to me, I had developed an attachment to 'my' guest. I did not want any harm to befall him. I as such tried to rouse him from his slumber. But he did not even open an eye.

.

The cloud came closer and closer and the roars became louder. With increasing fear and desperation I tried to shake awake my blissfully unaware guest. It was like trying to move a mountain – a near impossible feat.

And just as the cloud came up to us and screeched to a halt, my fearful eyes, which were moving between the menacing cloud and my guest, saw a slight smile appear on the latter's face. I watched helplessly as he turned his head toward me, opened his eyes and winked!

.

Perplexed, I watched the proceedings as a spectator, realizing somewhere deep within me that, this was the momentous event we had all been waiting for – without know what it would be, of course.

From the cloud emerged a huge man. The word 'huge' did not do justice to him. For, not only was he big, he was extremely muscular, and well proportioned too. Strength emanated from each and every pore of his.

Bare-chested, the yards of cloth covering his lower body could not hide the strength in those legs which had not only kicked up a storm, but also laid waste a substantial portion of the dense forest. In one hand, he held a full grown and yet sadly uprooted tree, while his other hand wielded a mace with great ease.

As the cloud of dust gradually settled down, with most of it coating this man's body (was it in reverence or mere relief? I wonder...), I saw a look of surprise flash through his eyes. It was immediately replaced by one of irritation. Surprise at finding someone who had not moved out of his way, and irritation about the fact that the same person had not made way for him.

.

Courtesy and manners instilled in him as a child forbade him from crossing over a supine being. And ego forbade him from deviating from his chosen path.

My guest appeared oblivious to this as he continued to feign sleep, his face turned away from this man.

The man's irritation grew by leaps and bounds and soon morphed into anger. I could actually see his muscles flex as he let out a roar and waited for my guest to make way.

.

Nothing happened.

.

And then, what followed was a conversation between... arrogance and commitment. The young and the ageless. Strength and power. The egoist and the wise. The hot-headed and the level-headed. The younger and the older.

.

"Move!"

.

No response. No movement. Not even a twitch.

.

"Move, old one!"

.

Again, no response.

"Move, you withered sack of bones!"

No response.

"Do you know who I am? The second of five. The mighty and powerful..."

"What would I know about might or power? *Old that I am.*" whispered my guest.

"Ah! So you speak. Move out of my way old one. I am on a mission."

"I too am on a mission child."

"Ha! What mission can an old one like you hope to accomplish? Move! I have a long way to go."

"I have come a long way to accomplish my mission. Of meeting you, my child."

"I am pleased to know that you wanted to meet me. Are you happy now? What other mission can one expect from a frail and helpless one like you? What will you know of missions anyway? You, who has not seen a city, let alone been part of a battle."

"I have moved mountains in my youth."

"Ha ha ha! Old age has made you senile. The last one to move a mountain was MY brother! And you claim to have done it too, you liar!"

"Your brother?"

"Yes. My brother. Fathered by the one who is the breathe of life in all. My brother - an ardent devotee of the greatest man to have ever walked on this planet. My brother – the one who moved mountains!"

"I am..."

"Wasting my time! Just because you belong to the same clan as him, you claim to have performed a near impossible feat? Shame on you! **Move out of my way right now before I do any harm to you!"**

"Sigh... I am old and helpless, and too tired to move. Why don't you just move away a little and walk by me?"

"Me? Change the path I have chosen to tread upon? Impossible! Make way for me old one. Before I lose my temper and hurt you."

"Well then. Why don't you move me a little to the side? You can carry on once you do that."

"You expect me to stoop to your level? Well, so be it. My mission is too important to be delayed any further. My wife will be eagerly awaiting my return with those divine smelling flowers."

Reluctantly, the man bent waist down and with a contemptuous scowl on his face and started to wedge a palm below the old one's waist so that he could lift him out of his way.

Nothing happened. Not a thing.

The powerful man, the mountain of a man who had uprooted trees and smashed to smithereens an entire stretch of a forest, could not insert even a single finger nail between the old one and the ground!

One palm gave way to two. Nothing happened.

The man sat down and exerted all his force – nothing happened. Well, nothing except that the old one smiled – I could see the smile. But the man could not.

"If you cannot move me, just push my tail away and walk on."

"Thank god. An easier option." thought the man and set about attempting to move the tail. The tail that had burnt down an entire city! How foolish was he.

Repeated failed attempts and a totally drenched-in-sweat torso finally made the once arrogant man see the truth.

With total humility, the man prostrated before the old and wise one and sought his introduction.

The wise one stood up and hugged his brother. The two were meeting for the first time.

And after repeated entreats from his younger brother, the ageless one started revealing his true self.

And what a sight it was!

He grew and grew and grew. And kept growing. From not even two feet in height, in the blink of an eye he grew bigger than the biggest tree in the forest. And in the next he grew taller than the nearby hills. The radiance that surrounded him had to be seen to be believed. So bright was he that it was as if thousands of suns had all concentrated in one place.

Blessed that we were, we could see it. But the man – his brother, on whose request the powerful one had started growing thus - could not physically bear to view this kind of growth. With utmost respect, he requested the knowledgeable one to reduce his size to a more 'normal' level which he did.

.

The two brothers hugged each other again. And then, the younger one listened to the older one's advise and instructions for that was the reason the wiser one had chosen to block his way.

.

Too soon came the time when the two had to part, which they did with great reluctance.

But the parting was filled with anticipation. For the elder promised the younger that he would be with the latter's brother at the time of the most crucial battle of all times – the mother of all wars that was to take place shortly.

.

Each went his way.

.

As for me, what can I say? Due to the grace of a primate, my fruit will remain dear to the family members of both brothers. Always.

XXIV
The Relief

I am jealous!

Envious. And a little upset. Maybe a little angry too.

We are five brothers. By right, all of us should have been part of the most talked about event of recent times, and maybe of times to come too. And yet...

Only one has been chosen!

One who is all air and sound! The rest of us, who are sheer substance, have been totally sidelined. Ignored. Put away.

We were neither consulted or informed. That our services would not be utilized was made known to us only when our Master shared that information with a friend.

We have been serving our Master faithfully for a very long time now. And yet, all of us except one, have been excluded from an arena where we could have probably put up our best display ever, and so easily brought down many others.

I do not know if my other siblings feel the same way as me. I will as such refrain from talking much about them. Rather, I am going to be selfish here, and vent out my feelings and frustrations.

.

For long, I have been an integral part of almost all of my Master's forays and missions. Each and every time that I have been summoned, I have delivered. Without fail.

So wonderful is the communication between us that no words need be spoken. He does not even have to call out to me. I am usually there, right next to him. And when I am not near him, a mere hand signal is sufficient for me to know that he is going to need my services. Most often, the very second he thinks of me, I know. In such cases, I am there with him, in a flash, ready to do as ordered. I have faithfully and consistently delivered – each and every time.

And now... when I could have been in top form doing as he commands, what does he do? He does not involve me! And chooses that empty headed one instead!!!

.

So here I am, watching, waiting, hoping...

.

Oh, what a scene this is! Filled with power and pathos. Strength and valour. Friendship and faith. Youth and age. Arrogance and commitment.

My master with his friend, and the aged one. In one place. Doing what they are destined to do – challenge each other.

So fast is the aged one, that he appears to be a moving blur. Or, considering all the damage he has wrought so far, comparing him with a hurricane may be more apt.

My Master's friend is no match to the old man's prowess. Or maybe, he is a little hesitant. I do not know.

•

But what I do know is that my Master is getting restless. I suspect that a thought may have taken root in his mind that, if things continue in this vein, he may not be able to fulfill a promise he made to a lady. That must be causing him to become angry, for he is one who honours his promises, each and every one of them.

My not being deployed too has been a promise he made, much to my grief. And that promise seems to be irking him now.

Most of the times that I have been of service to him, he has been very clinical in his approach, and often loving too. This is the first time I am seeing him so angry! Dare I presume that his anger is because I am not with him right now?

•

That thought is sheer impudence on my part! Oh, how could I even entertain such a thought? Even if it were for a mere second?

The truth is that he does not need me or any of us. He alone can take care of anything and everything. Like he did while protecting a young boy from his father's wrath a long time ago. That we are included in his deeds is our fortune.

•

"Forgive me Master for thinking so."

•

Wait! What is happening here?

•

My Master is enraged beyond belief. He is shaking in uncontrollable anger. And... he has summoned me!

•

Joyous, I rush to his side and take the place allocated to me. I know what is expected from me. And for the first time, I am having mixed feelings. I am glad that I am finally getting a chance to do what I am good at. I am eager to do what needs to be done.

But the eagerness is tempered with a tinge of sorrow for I am about to slay a person who is the most respected of all in recent times. A man so firm in his word that he is synonyms with the word 'Oath'. And it is because of such a man that my Master is going to break his word.

Oh! How ironical!

Even as I am pondering thus, many things happen simultaneously.

My Master readies himself to issue the command. Even as he is about to take action, his friend latches on to my Master's feet, while the aged one has put down his armaments and is now standing in all his glory, his confidence and well-deserved pride forming a glow around him.

On one side I can hear the friend beseeching my Master to remember his promise and spare the life of the aged one. I can also hear the aged one addressing my Master, declaring that he is ready to die right this moment, and would, in fact, consider himself blessed if my Master were to use me against him in this great battlefield.

The air all around us vibrates with my Master's rage, his friend's plea, and the aged one's strong and calm words.

On my part, I am trembling – with both eagerness and despair. I consider myself blessed, because I am finally going to clash with a noble soul - all others that I have killed have been wicked, cruel or vile. At the same time, I also feel sad that I may play a part in such a noble soul losing his life.

.

My Master hesitates. Maybe he has finally come out of the rage that briefly shrouded his thinking. Maybe he is finally listening to what his friend, and the aged one are saying. Maybe he has remembered his promise to not take up any arms in this Epic War.

.

Whatever the reason may be, my Master lowers his arm, and dismisses me.

I retract.

.

I am still sad that I will not be a part of the greatest war fought. And yet, I am very glad that my Master did not break his word. Or use me to take the life of the aged one.

.

Since times immemorial, I have been washed by the blood of many. But I shall always be thankful that I am not tainted with the blood of a noble soul. For it would have been a black mark on me. And my Master...

Sudarshana Chakra

XXV
The Separation

We love our brother.

More than ourselves, truth be told. He is the eldest, and the one we are close to. An open secret here - I am closer to my brother as compared to our other two siblings.

Back to our brother. Since I can remember, we have gone through all the ups and downs in our lives together. Happy moments or sad ones, we have faced them as one. Be it the painful betrayal by a loved one or the joyous occasion of a personal triumph, we have always stood by each other.

No force has been able to separate us, till now.

Our brother is very stubborn. Once he makes up his mind, no one can change it. The right decision or the wrong one, he will go ahead and do what he thinks needs to be done. This aspect of his character is what is unacceptable to our siblings who are twins. They have tried to counsel him many a time. They have often attempted to filter away some of the information or news that were meant for his ears alone. In vain, at times. When it has not suited him, he has simply ignored them. But that has not stopped them either. They just continue advising him.

I find this ongoing skirmish between them endearing. But the truth is, when it comes to others versus him, we – the three of us – will always be with him, and him alone.

•

As for me, I am very clear that the sole purpose of my existence is to protect him at all times. So attuned am I to him since childhood that we do not need words to communicate with each other. A mere touch is enough for me to gauge his moods and feelings.

Be it the day he was accepted as a pupil by the greatest master of all time. The moment he stood up to fight against what he perceived was wrong. The time when he made new friends. The second he was attracted to a beautiful lady. The occasion when vengeance was his. All those altercations between him and others who did not trust him. That moment of betrayal ... I remember each and every one vividly.

•

Life has not been kind to my brother. He has morphed from being an innocent child into a powerful person albeit one filled with anger. Despite all that, he is one with a large heart, and also probably the most misunderstood person of recent times.

And today, he is fighting a war on behalf of his friend. Leading from the front.

•

We are so proud of him. And so glad to be with him at this stage in his life. I can say without the least bit of arrogance that, as long as we are all together, no one can defeat us. So powerful are we...

•

Who is that I see coming towards us? He looks like an old Brahmin, weak, poor...Yet...

•

I sense trouble! The mere sight of this man is making me uncomfortable. It is as if he is the harbinger of death.

•

Shyly, or should that be slyly, he approaches our brother, and, ignoring us, he begs for alms – of his choice, knowing fully well that our brother will not refuse him whatever he asks. And this sly man, this masquerader, asks for ... us!

And our beloved, foolish brother ... smiles! As if he was expecting such a demand...

•

Knowing what is coming next, we desperately cling to him. Refuse to let go. Try to hang on. Yet, with the smile still playing on his lips, though his heart is heavy with sorrow, our brother forcibly tears us from him. Pulls us away from him.

The pain is horrendous. But I am sure that the pain our brother is going through at this moment is incomparable, beyond description. Drenched in blood and tears of regret, he hands us over to the one who asked for us. In return for this sacrifice he gets one solitary weapon which will only cause him more grief later.

Of what use is that weapon anyway? For our beloved brother is cursed. And without us, he will not live to see another day.

•

As we part, all the injustices done to him come to mind. Being abandoned by his own mother. Being labelled as one of lowly birth. Not being able to wed the one he desired. Being shunned by the elders. Being blatantly used by his so-called friends. And just now, being cheated of life by his half-brother's father...

.

We cry out in despair. And helplessness.

.

He alone can hear us. He looks at us one last time. And walks away.

.

No one will shed tears for our brother – the generous man, a valiant warrior and a cheated hero...

.

ꕤ

XXVI

The Dispatch

I am my friend's confidant, and probably one of the very few whom she trusts at this point of time.

.

She has just now poured out her heart to me. With nary an iota of shyness. No assumed coyness. No indirect allusions. Just the simple plain truth as she knows it.

Anyone else would probably chide her for the strong and, in a couple of places, uncomplimentary comparisons she has made. Others may even, with their voices tinged with sorrow or anger – depending on who is speaking, tell her that what she wants will not be.

But not me. In the short time that I have known her, my respect for her conviction and strength of character has grown by leaps and bounds. As also my admiration of her determination to get what she wants.

.

My friend has just now outlined her plan of action to me. And by doing so, has placed on me the immense responsibility of communicating the same to someone who she values more than life itself. I am now ready to set out on the most important mission of my life – the one I was created for, you may say. A mission that would, among other things, make or break relationships and probably result in battles too.

My mission is so critical that I cannot set out on my important journey unaccompanied. I have to be protected at all costs till such time that I complete the task assigned to me. Given this, you would be forgiven to think that I would be accompanied by a group of strong and able bodied men. And that is where you would be wrong.

Discretion being the better part of valour, I am placed in the care of a person who can, at best, be described as one of average build, maybe not very physically strong either. His intelligence and faith however are beyond doubt.

Together, we set out. We have a fair distance to cover, and very little time to do it in. The initial part of our journey proves to be a tricky one as we have to ensure that no one observes me accompanying my escort. I am as such covered from head to toe and smuggled out. After a few tense scenarios and having travelled without a break for hours, we reach our intended destination.

I can hear my companion speaking to another person – probably the one we have come to meet. While I am not able to see him yet since I am still covered, I can hear a rich melodious voice greet my escort and enquire about the purpose of our visit. The tone is well balanced, friendly and like music to my ears.

I am eager to see the person in whose company we now are. Propriety however forbids me from doing anything that will draw attention to me. But the wait...Oh, it seems so long! I am now starting to understand some of the things my friend shared with me earlier.

Finally, after what seems like hours but in reality is a few minutes only, my companion unmasks me and brings me forward saying, 'The message...'

.

The instant I get to see our host, all my fatigue and concerns about my friend are washed away. I am now in the presence of the most handsome man I have ever seen. Well built, a gentle smile on his lips, and a bewitching look in his eyes. One can keep looking at him for hours on end without blinking an eyelid, and melt in his love.

Our host gently pulls me to him and looks at me. I feel so weak-kneed in his presence that I would fold up if he were not holding me. I however do not forget my prime duty, that of communicating my friend's message to him.

As I go about discharging my duty, which is now both an honour and a privilege, I can sense the mood of my host. Joy at having received my friend's communication. Anger at what is happening. And finally a determination to do what needs to be done – exactly the same thing that my friend has requested.

.

Still holding me in his firm grip, the man rushes out of his room, without even taking leave of my companion. The last glimpse I have of my now erstwhile companion is that of a contended man – one who is happy to have discharged his duty effectively, and who is now sure that things will work out the way they have been planned.

The man I am with now rushes to his vehicle and sets off. His destination is clear - the place I came from.

.

The return journey is much faster.

.

As the sun sends down its rays to wash the earth, we reach the pre-appointed place. And wait for my friend to arrive.

.

Ah! There she is!

Coming out from one of the many abodes of this man's sister. Completely decked in the best finery of the land, looking like the glorious bride that she is.

The only thing missing is the smile on her face. She instead wears a slight frown, as if worried about something. I know the reason behind the worry. And I also know that in a very short while, her worries will be wiped away forever.

For he is here. Waiting for her.

.

The look of love in his eyes needs to be seen to be believed.

.

As if sensing his presence, my friend looks in the direction where we are currently stationed. And her face bursts into a smile the likes of which are impossible to replicate or describe. Leaving behind those accompanying her, my friend reaches us in a flash and takes over control of the transport we are currently in. Within seconds, and even as people start realizing what is happening, we are moving away, and towards the land of the man.

.

My friend's brother, and his good friend – the one with whom my friend was supposed to get married– follow with the intention of bringing her back. In vain though. What happens next is someone else's story, not mine.

All I know is that my friend is ecstatic to be with the man I accompanied on my return journey – a man who my friend had not seen till this day. But with whom she has had a relationship of the mind and the soul forever.

.

I am right now in a state of bliss. Happy that the purpose of my creation has been very satisfactorily achieved.

.

I am probably the first of my kind. There will be many after me. But people will not talk about them the way I will be spoken about, with reverence each time.

To tell the truth, I am also a little proud of the fact that none of my ilk will ever be able to match me in any manner whatsoever, for no one can serve two divine lovers the way I did.

.

. Rukmini's letter to Krishna .

XXVII

The Offering

No one wants us.

We come from a well-bred family. That should automatically get us respect, one would imagine. Unfortunately, with us, that is not the case.

Unlike our beautiful and healthy siblings, we are dry and lacklustre. So unwanted are we that we have been set apart from the rest, the intention is to get rid of us at the earliest.

The family we stay with does not care much for us. They believe that we will be of no use to them. The lady of the house is waiting for an opportunity to send us away – all she wants is a reason to do so, even if it is the flimsiest of all.

And that is exactly what is happening now. A poor gaunt lady, dressed in rags, has come to their doorstep, seeking help. The maid looks at us and decided that she has found an easy way to part with us. So off we are sent to service the destitute woman and her family.

A look of disappointment crosses her eyes when she first sets sight on us. It is immediately followed by one of resignation. Finally though, it is transformed into one of gratitude. What the reason for her gratitude is, we do not know. What we do know though is that she is very grateful to see us. With tears in her eyes, she murmurs a word of thanks in her feeble voice and sets off home.

.

Once we reach her house, we realize that our journey has just commenced.

The lady, with tears in her eyes, narrates her experience, while her husband looks at her and then us. His emotions and expressions mirror those of his wife – disappointment, resignation and then gratitude. He wipes the tears from his wife's eyes and tells her that he is ready to set out.

The lady throws a piece of rag over us for protection and hands over our charge to her equally indigent husband. And we set out on a tedious journey. By foot.

All of us huddle closer in an attempt to comfort each other. We do not know what awaits us at the end of this journey.

.

After a long arduous journey with nary a stop, we near a large stately house. Fearing that he would be ridiculed if we are discovered, the man hastily hides us. He then hesitantly approaches the gates of the house.

Those guarding it turn him away. He begs and pleads with them to let him in, in vain. So frail is he that he cannot even wrestle his way through. We can actually feel the sobs raking his malnourished body. Dejected, disappointed and disheartened, he starts to turn away. As we wonder about the reason for his disappointment, we hear a commotion nearby.

Since we are hidden, we are not able to see what is happening. But we can hear a cheerful voice exclaiming what must have been the man's name. He stops and turns around. And finds himself in a warm hug. He is now being led into the inner chambers of the house. Unknown to the guards, he has successfully managed to sneak us in too.

The air is becoming cool and fragrant. There are many subtle and nice sounds all around – a lady and a man speaking, distant sound of birds chirping, the strains of musical instruments accompanied by happy laughter...

Our curiosity has increased manifold by now. Finding a hole in the rag, I peep out. And what I see is... heart-warming! The man, the one we travelled with, is now seated on a throne, his demeanour reflecting a great deal of shyness and discomfort. A regally attired lady is standing next to him and fanning him. Kneeling at his feet is a dark-hued man, tenderly washing the man's feet with scented water.

As I watch, the dark-hued one sprays a few drops of that now dirty water onto his head!!! An honour that is reserved only for the elderly, and the very learned! The man we have accompanied is neither – he is just a poor Brahmin with many children, and a worried wife.

The husband and wife feed this man countless delicacies, the husband talking all the while, reminiscing about their adventurous childhood days together. The man we accompanied is so joyous that all he can do is smile and respond in monosyllables.

And then, all of a sudden, the dark-hued one asks the man, “Have you come empty-handed to see me? Without a single gift?”

.

As the man hesitates, the friend suddenly spots the rag thrown over us. He reaches out and snatches it from the man. Stuttering, the man tries to explain that he could not find any gift worthy of his glorious friend. The latter pays no head. He opens the tiny rag and finds us...

.

With a delight filled exclamation, “My favourite!!! And you were hiding it all this while. How could you?”

.

The friend scoops a handful of us and pops us into his mouth. And we are now in the mouth of the man, who as a child, showed his mother the entire universe in this very same mouth!!!

.

As the dark-hued one reaches out for another helping, his wife stops him with a twinkle in the eye and asks for a share for herself and the others. The rag and its contents are handed over to her, albeit reluctantly.

.

A flash of insight reveals to us that the man who brought us to his friend is, the very instant we were placed into that divine mouth, blessed with fortune that would last countless generations – he and his family will never go hungry again.

.

It gladdens us that we have played a small part in this wonderful story of true friendship that transcends time and wealth.

.

The bonus, or should we say 'blessing', is that forever hereafter, we shall be known as the favourite food of the lord. In addition, many will associate us with the name of his friend who brought us this fame.

Avalakki aka Kuchela Bakshana

The Answers You May Be Seeking

Hope you have enjoyed reading the stories. Given below are the incidents from which these stories have been derived.

1. The Birth - this story is about the battle that took place between a young boy created by Parvati, and Lord Shiva, who was unaware of the former's existence. It ends with the boy getting the head of an elephant and being called Vighnaharata.
2. The Sacrifice - following the death of Sati, Shiva goes into deep penance to the exclusion of everything else. This causes the Gods to worry as they await the son of Shiva who will destroy Tarakasura. Manmatha, the god of love, is sent to break Shiva's penance. This story focuses on Manmatha's thoughts during this incident.
3. The Beginning - this narration is from the perspective of the male Krouncha Pakshi which was shot down by a hunter as it waited for its mate. Maharshi Valmiki (he who wrote the Ramayana) witnessed this, and in grief uttered the first ever known couplet (or so it is believed).
4. The Con - narrated by the Yama paasha, this story is about how Savitri gets her husband's life back from Yama, the god of death.
5. The Cover - this story is narrated by the egg shell within which Garuda, Lord Vishnu's mount, developed. It alludes to the rivalry between the sisters Vinata and Kadru who were both married to the sage Kashyapa. Kadru used her sons, the naagas (snakes) to cheat Vinata who had to then serve as her slave.
6. The Elevation - this is the story of the destruction of Hiranyakashipu by Narasimha as narrated by the

threshold on which Narasimha sits and kills the demon.

7. The Purge - narrated by Parashurama's Axe, this story is about Parashurama killing the sons of Kartiviryarjuna who destroyed his family.
8. The Purification - this story is about the descent of Ganga to earth. It is written from three different perspectives interwoven into a single tale – the cursed forefathers of Rama in the form of ashes, the river Ganga, and Bhagiratha who ensured that Ganga reached earth and helped his forefathers attain salvation.
9. The Obeisance - this story is about Rama breaking the Shiva Dhanush (bow) at Sita's Swayamvara. It is narrated from the perspective of the bow.
10. The Crossing - the Lakshman rekhe narrates this story.
11. The Indicator - the battle between Vali and Sugreeva as narrated by the garland worn by the latter so that Rama would be able to identify the two correctly.
12. The Wait - this story is about the agony many undergo as they wait for Rama to return from exile (Vanavasa). It is narrated by the Rama Paduka (footwear of Rama that was brought to Ayodhya by Bharata and placed on the throne).
13. The Games - the various attempts by Kamsa to kill Krishna
14. The Release - narrated by the grinding stone, this story is about Krishna freeing the Yamalarjuna twins who were cursed to be on earth as trees till Krishna released them.
15. The Cleansing - River Yamuna shares her pain, and subsequently the blissful experience, when Krishna overpowers the serpent Kaali who was residing in her and troubling the villagers.
16. The Shower - this story is about Krishna curbing the arrogance of Indra by getting the villagers to pray to

the Govardhana Mountain rather than him. This story, which culminates with Krishna lifting the mountain with ease and sheltering the villagers beneath, is written from the perspective of a cloud that attempts to rain on Krishna with the intention of making him drop the mountain he has been holding up for seven days now.

17. The Lovers - The divine love between Radha and Krishna as narrated by her water pot and his flute.
18. The Avowal - this story is about that moment when Devavrata, the eighth son of Ganga and Shantanu, vows to never marry, so that his father can marry Satyavati aka Gandhavati. This oath of his gets him the name Bheeshma.
19. The Retrieval - the first meeting between Dronacharya and the Kuru princes as narrated by the ball the cousins were playing with.
20. The Gift - the severed thumb of Ekalavya narrates this poignant tale of gurudakshina sought by Dronacharya.
21. The Transgression - Draupadi's Locks narrate the incident where her Dushyasana drags her into the court of King Dhritarashtra and, along with others, humiliates her.
22. The Satiation - the Akshaya Patre gifted to the Pandavas by Surya narrates the incident when Rishi Durvasa and his disciples visit the forest during the Pandavas' vanavasa period and demand to be fed.
23. The Meeting - a banana tree narrates the epic meeting between Hanuman and Bhima when the latter is out looking for the Saugandhika pushpa.
24. The Relief - Sudarshana chakra shares his thoughts about the time when Lord Krishna broke his word of not taking up any arms in the Kurukshetra war and was about to attack Bheeshma who was fighting against

Arjuna.

25. The Separation - Narrated by Karna's kavacha (armour), it is about the incident during the Mahabharata war when a disguised Indra asks Karna to part with his kavacha and kundala (armour and ear ornaments) which were protecting him from the time he was born.
26. The Dispatch - the letter sent to Krishna by Rukmini.
27. The Offering - this story is about the friendship between Krishna and Sudama aka Kuchela, narrated by a grain of avalakki (flattened rice) that Sudama takes with him when he goes to meet Krishna.

9 798887 170855

Printed by Libri Plureos GmbH in Hamburg, Germany